CRAZY WOMAN BLUES

'Oh, Streeter!' he called. 'Hold it!' I turned and walked over to the curb. He said, 'Need a lift?'

'No thanks, Lieutenant,' I said, 'Just thought I'd take a little walk in the park, count the squirrels, try to forget last night . . .'

'Hop in. I'll drop you at the park entrance.'

'Thanks anyway, Lieutenant. The walk'll be good for what ails me.'

'And what's that Streeter?'

Bulldog Sweeney, Terror of Evil-doers. He never let up. He had a way of making me feel as if he had me by the scruff of the neck. Actually, of course, it was the other way around. Bulldog Sweeney was slow. Let him clamp his jaws on a solid clue, however, and he'd tear a case apart.

'Like I told you,' I said, 'I need to forget last night.'

He didn't insist . . .

J. F. BURKE

Crazy Woman Blues

MAGNUM BOOKS
Methuen Paperbacks Ltd

A Magnum Book

CRAZY WOMAN BLUES
ISBN 0 417 03720 1

First published in Great Britain 1979
by William Constable & Co Ltd
Magnum edition published 1982

Copyright © 1978 by J. F. Burke

Magnum Books are published by
Methuen Paperbacks Ltd
11 New Fetter Lane, London EC4P 4EE

Made and printed in Great Britain
by Richard Clay (The Chaucer Press) Ltd,
Bungay, Suffolk

For Big Gray

1

All the acts had gone as rehearsed, or better, except the last bit, the finale of Doctor Caligari's magic show. The act closed with the disappearing-girl trick, and of course it was called *The Cabinet of Doctor Caligari*. The pretty girl goes into the cabinet. Caligari closes the door. He says some abracadabra, makes a few magic passes with his wand, opens the door of the cabinet, and behold! the pretty girl has vanished. He closes the door again, does some more mumbo-jumbo, opens the door, and *voilà!* she has reappeared.

But tonight she didn't reappear. Caligari closed and opened the door again and again. Still she didn't show. He was getting laughs, though. Then he had a brainstorm. While the audience was laughing, he came over to the piano, where I'd been playing background, and proposed a switch ending for the act.

"I'll go down to the greenroom," he said. "Something's got to be wrong with Alice." Our greenroom, where the performers prepare, or try to relax, is in the basement under the stage. "Give me ten seconds inside the cabinet,"

Caligari said. "Then have the stagehands dismantle it and take it off. Should be good for a laugh."

"You and Alice didn't cook this up since rehearsal," I said, "being the geniuses that you are?"

"On my mother's grave," he said, "I don't know what's with Alice."

I told him to try the switch ending. He went back to the cabinet. I caught the eye of my maître d', Dom Ambrosini, and while he came over I vamped some magic music for Caligari, spooky arpeggios in a minor key. He was starting his hocus-pocus with Latin-sounding phrases and mysterious wavings of his wand. I told Dom to have the stage manager dismantle and remove the cabinet as soon as I stopped playing. He went to speak to the stage manager.

Doctor Caligari now opened the cabinet and stepped inside. He closed the door. I played four chords in G minor, then stopped.

The stagehands came at once. When the audience saw the cabinet being taken apart and bundled up, the laugh came. Not from the belly, but good.

Of course Caligari and Alice weren't onstage to take their bows, so I went at once into my turn, a set of variations on "Mary Had a Little Lamb" à la Scott Joplin, Fats Waller, Thelonius Monk, and Duke Ellington. I was lousy, played nothing but clams, couldn't concentrate for worrying about Alice. She was a trouper, and she was ambitious. She wouldn't deliberately crab the act. I thought surely she must be lying hurt down in the greenroom, injured somehow by a failure of the trapdoor or the electric lift. That's how she vanished in the disappearing-girl bit. No mirrors, no double walls in the cabinet, no *real* illusion, merely a trapdoor.

But magic wasn't the point of the act. Alice was. She was a talented mimic and could do astonishingly realistic impersonations. This is what she did in *The Cabinet of Doctor*

2

Caligari. She entered the cabinet as herself, Alice the cigarette girl, which is what she was offstage. Her first reappearance was an impersonation of Greta Garbo, her second was Marlene Dietrich, and her third was Marilyn Monroe. Her transformations were uncanny. She'd be standing there as Alice, and suddenly you're looking at Garbo, or Dietrich, or Monroe. She could probably have done Eleanor Roosevelt.

On the payroll she was María de los Ángeles Farah Gómez. Her stage name was Alice, just plain Alice. Born in Veracruz, she said, of Spanish parents, she was raised in Mexico City, trained in theater arts at UCLA, and had come east about six months before.

After making the rounds of theatrical agents day after day for five months and getting nothing but patted on the ass, she came to Pal Joey's one afternoon. I held auditions in the afternoons on weekdays. I hired her as soon as I saw her act. She didn't have Caligari then. She just stood facing the audience, stage center, and ran through her impersonations without a word. It was unnerving, a kind of living Madame Tussaud's Wax Museum. But it lacked humor, so I put her with Doctor Caligari. She was what his disappearing-girl trick needed.

By one o'clock I had finished my set and bowed off. Caligari was coming in the street door, looking like a worried Dracula. I met him at the bar.

"Not a sign of Alice," he said. "She wasn't in the greenroom. I don't think she could have hurt herself. The trapdoor works fine. Nothing wrong with the lift. I went out through the garden and the alleyway. None of the waiters saw her leave. She's just gone. I don't understand it. I even looked in the kitchen and the ladies' rest rooms."

"Did you check her apartment?"

He said no. I said I would. I thought if she'd been taken ill suddenly she might have gone up to her place.

3

She lived on the third floor, just over the back half of my own apartment. Mine was the parlor floor of this old brownstone. At the time, I was renting the four apartments on the two top floors to the club's performers. She could have gone directly to her apartment by the inner stairway from the greenroom to the upper floors, bypassing the club.

I flew up the steps three at a time. I was about to press Alice's doorbell when I heard a loud thump inside the apartment and a man's voice cursing. A second man told him to shut up.

Since Alice lived alone, I stooped and looked through the keyhole. The apartment was dark, but I saw a light, a small one, flashing about the living room like a big firefly. So I tiptoed down to my apartment and got a set of master keys and my Walther P-38. Then I went silently up the stairs and very carefully, slowly slipped the keys into the tumblers and quietly turned the locks. There were three locks. As I worked I listened to the voices inside, a tenor and a baritone, speaking in stage whispers. I pressed my ear to the door and heard their dialogue quite clearly.

One of them said, "It isn't here. Just this goddamn knife and the ring." It was the baritone. His voice was rough; his manner brusque. His speech was American. He said, "She wouldn't keep it here anyway. She's not stupid."

"No, Charles, she's not stupid. She's crazy," the other man said. His voice had a nasal whine, a complaining sound. The accent was Italian of some kind. He said, "If you hadn't let her get away . . ."

Charles said, "Will you get off it? Christ Almighty, she spiked my instep! How was I to know she'd try an old trick like that? And how come *you* didn't do something? You carry a gun. Afraid to use it?"

"You were holding her, Charles. I couldn't risk it. I might have shot *you* instead, the way she was manhandling you.

4

Besides, I had all I could do myself, going through her handbag. The bitch wouldn't turn loose of it. She's not only crazy, Charles, she's a wildcat." The Italian accent was very clear and precise. I thought it was probably Roman. He said, "Anyway, I got her keys. And this wallet. Here, you hold them."

"Fat lot of good they are," Charles said. I heard the keys fall jingling to the floor and Charles grunting as he bent to pick them up. "Let's get out of here," he said. "We took the place apart, and it isn't here. Now she's gone too."

"We'll wait," said the Roman. "I believe it *is* here, Charles."

"You said yourself, she's isn't stupid. This is the last place she'll come now."

"I also said she's crazy. We wait."

"You wait, sit on your fat ass. I'm going to look for her. And I'm taking the ring, also the dagger, so it shouldn't be a total loss."

The Roman said, "You can stick it, *caro mio.*"

I flung the door open, reached around the edge of the doorway, and flipped the wall switch. In the sudden flood of light I saw a very tall man looming before me. He towered over me though I stand six-one. There was a second man, short and fat, and as I switched on the lights he ran into the kitchen.

The bedroom door was open. I saw nobody in there. The bedroom was dark, but I could see the window because of the lights outside, for the sky over midtown at night glows brightly enough to read by. The bedroom window curtains fluttered in the night breeze. I did not observe more; the tall man was rushing me.

As he came at me his right hand reached for his hip. I didn't intend to shoot until I saw his gun. That should have left me enough time, but it was nearly a fatal mistake. As he closed in, his left hand swung sharply sideways, striking

5

my gun arm, and the gun flew out of my hand. I heard it skitter across the floor.

What he'd reached for on his hip was not a gun but a knife, a big one. He jabbed it straight for my ribs, holding it flat. He knew how. I crowded into him, grabbed his wrist, twisting his forearm downward and his knife hand upward so the blade pointed toward *his* ribs, not mine. He was bigger, but a professional pianist's hands and arms have tendons and sinews like wires. I got both hands on his forearm, forced his knife hand down below his rib cage, and shoved sharply upward. At the same time I heard a gunshot and felt the shock of the bullet striking his back. The impact drove his body toward me as I shoved the knife home. He screamed once, then loosed his grip on the hilt. I stepped back. He fell on his side, doubled up and gasping.

I looked around for the second man and saw him coming out of the kitchen. He was holding a small-caliber automatic. I thought I'd had it then, for if I rushed him he'd shoot me. I couldn't understand why he didn't shoot anyway. Had I turned to run out of the doorway, he could have shot me in the back. So I really had no choice but to go for my gun. It lay on the floor in a far corner. I went for it, never expecting to reach it. By the time I'd got it, the other man was going through the bedroom doorway.

I had one good look at him as he slammed the door shut. It was enough. He was short, very fat, had a moon face with big, bulging pale eyes, pasty white skin, tiny red rosebud mouth, nose wide and short like a snout, hair long and lank and gray. Not a face you'd soon forget. He looked familiar, and I have good visual recall, but there wasn't time to search my mind.

I heard him turn the lock in the bedroom door. I gave it a second's thought, considered the corpse named Charles, and figured I might need that fat little man, dead or alive, to help me explain things like the bullet in Charles's back. I pegged three quick shots through the bedroom door panels. So did the fat Roman. I fell prone and waited. He didn't cry out, and I didn't hear him fall, so I got up and shot the lock out of the door and rushed in. He was gone. Up or down the fire escape.

If he came off the fire escape in the garden, one of the waiters would nab him, unless he started shooting. I poked my head out of the window and took a quick look upward, ready to dodge a bullet, but I saw nobody. I climbed out of the window and sprinted up the fire escape, and when I reached the top I saw him trying the rooftop door of the next brownstone. He backed off from it. I tried to draw a bead on him. He shot the lock out of the door. In the very poor light I couldn't chance a shot, maybe sending a wild one into the night. You can read a newspaper by the glow of light over Times Square, but picking off a man at twenty yards with a 5-inch barrel is chancy.

I might have gone after him, but he had a good lead and he was fast on his feet. Fat men can be very nimble. Anyhow, it was a police matter. I watched him go through the rooftop doorway.

I went down the fire escape to Alice's apartment. Nine-millimeter rounds make a very loud noise, but I heard nobody in the hallway. Nor had I really expected to, since everyone who lived on the top floors also worked in the club, which is where they were supposed to be at the moment. The hall door stood wide open. I closed it. The pungent smell of gunpowder hung heavy in the room.

The tall man lay on his side by the door, curled up around a pool of blood. A fine Mexican throw rug was ruined. His grip on the knife had relaxed, of course, but the long blade remained sticking in him up to the hilt. I felt his jugular. No pulse. The eyes were half open, the pupils wide and dark. The small bullet hole in the back of his jacket, well below the right shoulder, near the center seam, had oozed very little blood.

I studied the knife. More correctly, it was a dagger. It had a guard of gold and an ivory hilt set with star sapphires. Not a fighting weapon and hardly the sort of blade a man would wear in this age of the switchknife. I lifted the dead man's coattail over his right hip, looking for a scabbard. Instead I found a small, razor-thin cut in the pants belt where he'd apparently stashed the dagger, sticking it in between belt and trousers. Antique daggers don't usually have the quality of metal needed for such a keen edge. I recalled that the blade had gone into him very smoothly. Toledo steel was my guess. I wanted to pull it out and examine it further.

Then I noticed the ring on his little finger, left hand, rubies set in platinum filigree on a rose gold band. Not a man's ring. Charles had said he was taking the ring and the dagger "so it shouldn't be a total loss," meaning that what they'd come looking for, and failed to find, was much more valuable than either the dagger or the ring. The fat Roman, too, had implied as much. How had he put his contempt for the ring and the dagger? "You can stick it, *caro mio.*" If rubies and sapphires were small change, what had they been looking for?

Versatile Alice, girl of many faces. Charles and the fat Roman had known one of her faces that I'd never seen. How could a 19-year-old girl get herself involved in a jewel scam? But then, I thought, why not? In show business you meet some pretty precocious youngsters. Or maybe it was all a gross mistake and she was taking the rap for somebody else. Or she did have something valuable, but she didn't know it. Obviously I was trying to get her off the hook, in my own mind, and I knew I couldn't. She was up to her lovely tush in this thing, whatever it was. If she didn't have what the burglars were after, they certainly had reason to believe she had it, for in fact she did have the jeweled dagger and the ruby ring.

But whatever the real nature of her involvement, I intended to do whatever I could to help her. I'd known Alice only a month. I wanted to know her much longer.

I went through the rooms and found contents of drawers and closets tossed, bed taken apart, mattress slashed, a divan completely gutted. It was much worse than I'd noticed in the heat of battle. They'd even ransacked the kitchen, emptying cans of coffee, sugar, and flour on the floor. The doors of the oven and the dishwasher hung open. I checked the bathroom. So had the burglars.

I returned to the dead man, knelt by him, and went through his pockets. He had two key cases. One belonged to Alice. The other did not, unless she had a car I didn't know about. There was a wallet. In it I found three hundred and some dollars in cash and a California driver's license issued to Terence D. Moran. I checked the license code for Moran's description and saw that it was oddly similar to Charles's. Same general age. Approximately the same height and weight. But Moran's eyes were brown, according to the license code, and Charles's eyes were gray. I thought about it, then looked more closely at the dead man's eyes. With my right index finger I tapped the nail against one of his eyes. No contact lens. So what was he doing with Terence D. Moran's license? It could have been used for ID, of course, if a cop didn't check it too closely. I pocketed the wallet, the license, and both sets of keys.

The aftereffects of the fight and the shooting were getting to me, and my hands were shaking pretty badly. I tried to concentrate on the problem: keeping Alice out of this as much as possible. I was going to have to call the police, and the jeweled dagger worried me. Not the ruby ring. I worked the ring off Charles's little finger and dropped it in my pocket. But to take the dagger . . . How in hell could I explain it? I left it where it was, up to its jeweled hilt in Charles.

I went over the apartment again, trying to find a clue to

what the burglars had been looking for. Whatever it was, it could have been concealed in a coffee or sugar can. Or at any rate the burglars had thought so.

It was one-thirty when I turned off the lights and went out into the hall, thinking about what I was doing: concealing evidence. But evidence of what?

As I was locking Alice's apartment, Herb Junep came down the stairs. He had the apartment directly above. He was our comic, but he hadn't performed tonight because his routines were too blue for family television. So said the producer. Though we opened at midnight, he said *some* families would be watching. Tonight was opening night of our first thirteen weeks on TV, with a longer run on prime time if the show went over. I hadn't fought the producer over Junep's act, because I agreed for my own reasons. Blue humor goes down all right in a café theater like Pal Joey's, where a lot of consenting adults are anonymously boozing, but it can be questionable taste on the television screen in a private home. I can think of other ways to look at it, but that's mine. Anyway, I'd thought Junep was downstairs watching the show. Right now he should have been with the other performers, fraternizing with the producer and the network executives. He was part of our ensemble, after all.

He said, "Hi, Joe! How'd it go?"

I said, "What?"

"The show," he said.

"Where in hell were you?"

"Watching it on my set."

"So why ask me how it went?"

"I missed the last act. Had to take a crap."

"Herb, you're an uncouth creep."

He smiled at me as if I'd paid him a compliment. Maybe I had.

"If I thought you meant that," he said, "I'd kiss you."

10

A lot of banter, and nothing about gunshots. How could he not have heard them? There was a niggling doubt at the back of my mind, for you couldn't tell what Herb Junep was thinking by what he said or the way he said it or by watching his face. He was an actor and a comic, always copping attitudes, ironic, satiric, sarcastic, or just plain deadpan dumb. If you told him you'd been struck by a speeding car, he'd say, "Make and model?" He was an ordinary-looking man in his late thirties, about five-eight, a hundred fifty pounds, nothing unusual about his appearance unless he chose to make it so. He had what's known in theater as the rubber face. In repose it was plain, an expressionless mass of putty, but in action it could assume any human emotion or combination of emotions. So, if he hadn't mentioned hearing gunshots there seemed no point in asking him directly. I was in no mood to play straight man. Anyway, why should he pay special attention to gunshots in New York City? Besides, this was the Fourth of July weekend, so it could have been cherry bombs.

I said, "Herb, there's been some trouble. Alice has disappeared. I came up to see if she was in her apartment, and I surprised some burglars. I had to kill one of them. He's in there now. The other got away. I'm going to call the police, but when they come I don't want them to know Alice is missing. I have my reasons, Herb . . ."

"To hear," he said, "is to obey."

"Go on down to the club," I told him. "Speak to Dom for me. Tell him what I just told you, and ask him to pass the word. Keep Alice out of it for the time being. Deaf-and-dumb if anybody should ask about her."

"I hope she's all right," he said.

We descended the stairs together. He asked no questions. He continued on down to the club. I went into my apartment.

2

I dialed 911, and a lady cop answered. "Police emergency," she said pleasantly. I told her there'd been a burglary and a homicide at Pal Joey's on West 50th Street. I said I was Joseph Streeter, owner of the club, and I'd be waiting for the police by the front door. She started to say something, but I hung up. She had all she needed.

I put my gun in the drawer of the nightstand by my bed, then thought better of it and got out a shoulder holster. I'd wear the piece, at least until I knew what was happening. My fingers were still shaking as I replaced the three rounds. The Walther P-38 holds nine shells, eight in the clip and one in the chamber. I lowered the hammer and set the safety.

As I went down to the club I tried to gather my thoughts. The dagger and the ring were worth quite a lot of money. I know gem values fairly well, and it seemed to me that the stones alone, the star sapphires on the hilt of the dagger and the rubies in the finger ring, could add up to five big figures, maybe six. I have the feeling, which is probably universal, that jewel scams, like intelligently managed bank robberies, are not so much crimes (except in a pettifogging legalistic sense) as they are a sharing of the wealth. If Alice had something more valuable than rubies and sapphires, I wanted her to keep it. And I wanted to keep her.

In the club I found the television crews relaxing. They couldn't clear out their cables and other equipment until the crowd thinned out. The house was still packed. It was Saturday night of the long July Fourth weekend, and Pal Joey's was hotter than the hinges of hell though the air-conditioners were going full blast. The kleig lights had been burning like dozens of small suns for an hour. The room was one big sauna. Everyone was sweating, performers, TV crews, waiters, bartenders, cooks, and customers. No matter, it had been a great evening. The crowd had loved us. If we hadn't been on TV we would have done encores all night. Our customers included the city's leading nightlife commentators, several theatrical producers and impresarios, and their stars from other shows. Café theater certainly isn't new in this country, but the quality hasn't often been good, so this was a big night not only for Pal Joey's but for theater at large.

Pal Joey's had been a straight nightclub until my partner died. Well, not so straight. He'd had card rooms upstairs. But after his demise I changed the club to cabaret, or café theater, with a revolving stage, theatrical lighting, a custom-built sound system, and so forth. We offered improvisational theater, skits and blackouts, and variety acts, dancers, singers, comics, magic shows. And my jazz. Pal Joey's had originally been built around my piano. I'd been able to realize a dream that all jazz pianists have: to own their own club, featuring their kind of jazz. I'd had a big blue neon sign put up over the street door, a kangaroo—a *joey,* as they say in Australia—wearing a top hat and playing a grand piano. No, I don't wear a top hat myself.

13

Jazz gets people together, and soon after I opened the club, unemployed musicians and singers began sitting in. Other performers, dancers, actors, comics, soon followed. It was showcase theater. I put a few of them on the payroll, and it was full-fledged cabaret. But then along came Jock Alfieri, a jazz buff with money, and he wanted to make an investment and change Pal Joey's into a big, posh night-club. With card rooms upstairs. As it happened, I was leasing the building at the time, and when Jock showed up with the title in his hand, making him my landlord, I went along. We became partners. Later I learned that my real landlord was his uncle, Rocco Lucarelli, a well-known mafioso. Any-how, Jock got himself into big trouble with a bad Greek and was killed, to make a long story short, and I then shut down the card rooms, bought the building from Uncle Rocco's widow, and turned Pal Joey's into the café theater, or caba-ret, that it should have been all along. The killing had precipitated a gang war between Rocco Lucarelli and Gen-tleman John Volos, resulting in the decease of both, along with several of their henchmen. *R.I.P.*

Pal Joey's wasn't a big club, being only the garden floor and patio of an old brownstone, but it was a beautiful room. Two walls were mirrored with pier glass, so the room looked enormous. All the woodwork was old, solid mahog-any. The chandeliers were antique crystal. I had semicircu-lar tables built, so guests could dine and watch the show with nobody's back to the stage. Our crowning glory was Dom Ambrosini, my maître d', an artist who conducted the staff like Stokowski directing a symphony orchestra. He hired only European chefs and waiters. As I entered the club he came up to me. He bowed ever so slightly, from the hips.

"Mr. Junep told me about the trouble upstairs, sir."

"Any word of Alice?"

14

"No, sir. Mr. Morgenlicht and his guests have been asking for her."

Heinz Morgenlicht, the television producer of our Saturday midnight show, bossed only the shooting setup. The show itself was the ensemble's production. I watched production costs, of course, but the direction was *tout ensemble.* In fact, we didn't even have an M.C. Didn't need one. Each of us knew what to do. I didn't think the television crews needed Morgenlicht, either, but the studio executives did. He and they were being entertained now at my private table by the evening's performers. Except of course for Alice.

"Tell them she's having a *crise de nerfs* and she's gone down to the Jersey Shore for a few days," I said, loudly enough for anyone nearby to hear. "Strain of a first night," I added. "Nothing serious. She'll be here for Thursday's rehearsal."

"I am so glad," Dom said. "We were worried."

Quietly I added, "That's for Morgenlicht and his people. I don't know where Alice is or why she split. Keep it confidential for the moment, Dom. I called the police and reported a burglary-homicide, but I didn't mention Alice's disappearance. Let's try and keep it that way until I learn what's happening."

"Yes, sir. Will there be anything else, Mr. Streeter?"

"Just make sure the staff and performers understand, I want nothing but deaf mutes where Alice is concerned."

Sirens were shrieking all over Times Square as I went to the street door. I listened to their maniacal howling and lit a cigar with trembling fingers. Old Matt Griffin, our doorman, formerly a night clerk at the Hotel Commodore, told me that Dom had already informed him as instructed. Matt looked as worried as if his own daughter had gone astray. In this neighborhood that would be some straying.

"So where you think she went to, Joey? Somebody snatch her, or what?"

Matt was about seventy, but except for white hair he looked twenty years younger. He was a hot jazz trumpeter until he went into the hotel business in order to eat regularly, and when the Commodore closed, the year before, I hired him. He could double as bodyguard if needed, for he could shoot your hat off with any kind of handgun at thirty yards and part your hair without scratching your scalp. Once a month we went to the Broadway Rifle and Gun Club and plinked targets. Matt was not only a dead shot, he was fast as a bat. As for the trumpet, he still had a fine lip and occasionally sat in with me. We looked enough alike to be father and son, both of us being tall, long-jawed, and white haired, though my hair color is due to a tropical fever I caught many years ago in Brazil.

"I don't think she was snatched," I told him. "But I don't really know what to think, Matt. One thing sure, she's in trouble. I want you to take a walk down the block and speak to some of the boys. See if Nickels and Mister Magoo are in McAnn's. Pass the word, find Alice."

I watched him walk down the block. If Alice were still in the area some of the street characters would know it, for there are no secrets around Times Square unless you're a stranger.

A city car with its cherry light flashing, but no siren, pulled in to the curb, followed by screaming squad cars pouring into the block from both ends. I knew the cop behind the wheel of the city car, Lieutenant Aloysius Sweeney of Homicide. He'd been in charge of the case when my partner got aced a year earlier. He was a sergeant then. That homicide made him a lieutenant. He sat behind the wheel, talking on the radio, so I waited. When he'd finished I walked over to the car.

He got out smiling and took my hand. He was a cocky little man with bright brown eyes, bushy red moustache, and craggy eyebrows, and he spoke with a brogue as thick as the bogs he came from. Though his manner was often abrasive, he was a gentleman. It's hard to be a cop and remain a gentleman, but in Homicide it can be done, for the temptations come rarely if ever.

"Glad to see you're all right, Streeter," he said. He glanced at his wristwatch. It was one-forty. Uniformed cops and detectives in plainclothes were standing around awaiting orders. He took me to one side. "What happened, Streeter?" I said I'd killed a burglar in self-defense in an upstairs apartment. He told a sergeant to post men around, inside and outside the club, and wait for further orders. "What floor, Streeter?" I said third floor back. "That's where we'll be," he told the sergeant. And to me he said, "Lead the way."

I led him up the front steps. Some detectives followed us. When we got to the parlor floor landing, Sweeney had to pause and catch his breath. He was in his fifties, and spry enough, but he'd picked up some weight in the past year.

"I'll never live to make captain," he wheezed. "The lieutenant's easy life has turned me soft." I think it was supposed to be a joke. On the third floor landing he had to rest again. I wondered how long since he'd had a medical. He leaned heavily on the banister. "This thing tonight," he said. "Does it have something to do with what happened here last year?"

There seemed to be nothing about tonight's events that could possibly tie into my late partner's demise. The big bad Greek who put out the contract on him was dead, and so were several of his gang. As for my late partner's family, Uncle Rocco himself was the only one who might have had a continuing interest in me or my club. I had paid his widow a good price for the building, and the Lucarellis were satisfied. So last year's murders were definitely a closed file. But I thought I saw a way to point Sweeney away from Alice.

17

"My late partner was into things I never suspected," I said. "It could be something coming up now that we overlooked then."

"Like what?"

"Well, Uncle Rocco had a very large family. So had Gentleman John."

"You're saying a vendetta? You think the families found out you set up Uncle Rocco and Gentleman John?"

"I didn't exactly set them up," I told Sweeney. "I sort of stage-managed the confrontation. It would have happened anyway, though not the way it happened."

"A whole year later," Sweeney said. He cocked a brown beady eye at me, leaned on the banister, and stroked his moustache. "Sure," he said. "But first the facts." He straightened up. "Is this the apartment?" I said it was and took the set of master keys out of my coat pocket. "In a minute," he said. "Whose apartment is this? Who lives on these upper floors?"

"This one," I said, "is Alice's. She's an actress. The one down the hall is Doctor Caligari's. He's a magician. On the top floor, Stacy Brown and Colleen Costello have the front apartment. Stacy's our jazz singer. Colleen's a dancer. The top floor rear apartment is Herb Junep's. He's our comic."

"Heard of him," Sweeney said. "Now this Doctor . . . What's the name?"

"Doctor Caligari."

"That his real name, or his stage name?"

"His real name's John Radulovich."

"Russian?"

"Montenegrin."

"He's colored?" He said it with a straight face. I didn't reply. "All right," he said. "I'm not prejudiced. Just asking. Let's go in."

I unlocked Alice's door and we went in. The rooms were just as I'd left them, looking like a battleground. The corpse lay where it had been, though not quite in the same position. When I'd last seen it, the body had been lying curled up on its side. Now it lay on its back. And the knife was gone.

Sweeney stood just inside the doorway, looking around. Seeing how the apartment had been tossed, he whistled. He studied the corpse, the large knife hole in its midriff, and the wide pool of blood. Charles was a big man, and he'd bled a lot.

"Well, now," Sweeney said, looking up at me from under the craggy red eyebrows. "You didn't tell me you did it with a knife, Streeter. How come?"

"I don't know, Lieutenant. After-shock maybe. My nerves are still jangling. My head feels like . . . I know I've lost my cool. It'll come back. About the knife, he attacked me with it, we fought, I turned it on him."

"So where is it?"

"Lieutenant, believe me," I said, "I left it sticking in him. He was lying on his side when I locked up the apartment and went downstairs to call Nine-one-one." I pointed out a smear of blood on the dead man's coatsleeve. "Whoever took the knife," I said, "first wiped off the blood. Apparently he had to turn the body over on its back to pull the blade out. It was a big two-edged blade."

I didn't mention the star sapphires set in its golden hilt. So far as Sweeney knew, this caper had nothing to do with jewels.

He was looking around the room as I spoke. He saw the bullet holes in the bedroom door, turned toward the living room wall opposite the door, and saw three more. But there were six in the door panels.

"You and this man fought for the knife," he said, "and you managed to turn it on him and kill him with it. So what about those bullet holes?"

"There was a second burglar," I said. "He got away. We

19

exchanged a few shots as he was leaving, random shots through the bedroom door."

"Describe him, please."

Whoever the fat Roman was, he knew Alice, and presumably she knew him. They knew each other through a jewel scam of some kind, but until I knew what Alice's role was, I thought I'd better find the fat man before Sweeney did.

"Sorry," I said. "In all the confusion, I didn't get a good look at him."

"Not very clear, Streeter. You'd better tell me from the beginning what happened. How did you come to discover burglars in this apartment?"

I said, "Well, to the best of my recall it was like this. After the show I thought I'd go up to the roof and smoke a quiet cigar. It's restful up there on a clear night like this. I've built a sundeck . . ."

"Get on with it, Streeter."

"Yes. Well, I was tired and keyed up. It's been a strain, you know, getting tonight's program ready, our first night on television . . ."

"I saw part of the show," Sweeney said. "Let's get to the homicide, shall we?"

"Sorry. I seem to have the usual first-night jitters, and then on top of that, this killing . . ."

"Come *on,* Streeter!"

"Yes. Well, on my way up to the roof, as I was passing this apartment, I heard two men's voices inside. Since the tenant lives alone, I thought I'd better investigate. So I went and got the master keys and my gun. When I let myself into the apartment, one of the burglars jumped me, knocked the gun out of my hand, and pulled a knife. We struggled. His partner had run into the kitchen when I came in. While the man with the knife and I were struggling, the one in the kitchen cranked off a shot and caught his partner in the back. If you'll turn the body over . . ."

Sweeney did so and saw the bullet hole. He nodded, and I continued. "When the man in the kitchen saw his partner fall, he ran into the bedroom, heading for the window and the fire escape. He shut and locked the bedroom door before I could retrieve my gun, but when I got it I pegged three shots through the door, hoping for a lucky one. He fired three in return. Then I shot the lock off the door and went in after him, but he was already gone, up the fire escape. I followed and got to the roof in time to see him shooting the lock off the rooftop door of the next brown-stone. I couldn't risk a shot at that range, the light was too poor. I didn't think I could catch him, so I came back down and phoned Nine-one-one."

"You came back down by way of the fire escape, and you reentered the apartment through the bedroom window?"

"That's right."

"Was the hall door open or closed all this time?"

"Open."

"And the knife, was it still in the body when you came back down from the roof?"

"Yes."

"Quite a bundle. You're lucky the gunman hit his partner instead of you. Very lucky. May I see your gun?" I handed it to him. "Same piece you had a year ago?"

I said it was, and the same license. He gave it back. Stepping around the corpse, he went over to the bedroom door and examined the bullet holes, three big ones and three smaller ones. Then he went to the opposite wall of the living room and studied the fat Roman's bullet holes.

"Very, very lucky," he said as he came back to me. "The other man had a small-caliber gun, a twenty-five or a twenty-two. If he'd had a nine-millimeter cannon like yours, he'd have bagged both of you birds with one shot." To the other detectives he said, "Take a look around, see if you can find a clue to what the burglars were after." To me he said, "You wouldn't know, would you?" I said no. "The tenant keep valuables around?"

"I doubt it."

"Where is the tenant, by the way?"

"She left for the Jersey Shore right after tonight's performance, the last act."

"Her name?"

"María de los Ángeles Farah Gómez."

He got out a notebook and a ballpoint. I spelled it for him.

"She Spanish?"

"Mexican."

"What's she do here?"

"Just an actress."

"Where'd she go on the Shore?"

"Down to A.C."

"Atlantic City?" He wrote it down. "Where's she staying there?"

"She didn't say."

"When do you expect her back?"

"Thursday, for rehearsals of the next program. We're on every Saturday midnight for thirteen weeks."

"Describe her, please."

I didn't hesitate. He could meet her face to face and never recognize María de los Ángeles Farah Gómez or Alice the cigarette girl behind the living masks of Garbo or Dietrich or Monroe, or a dozen other famous women.

He put away his notebook and ballpoint and knelt by the corpse. He opened the mouth and examined the teeth.

"Lot of expensive work here," he said. "This was no poor man, and he didn't get rich burglarizing places like this one. White hands, manicured nails. Distinguished-looking bastard, isn't he? That suit would set me back a whole payday. Cashmere. Bit warm for this weather." He opened the jacket. "Paris label," he said. He stood up and stepped away from the body. He looked vaguely around the room, chewing his moustache and snapping his fingers. "That's it!" he said. "Streeter, did you leave the bedroom window open when you came back from chasing the other man?"

"Yes," I said. "I don't think I touched anything but the hall doorknob and the light switch."

"So whoever took the knife came in through the open window," he said. "The second burglar must have come back. Something about that knife could identify him, right?"

"Looks like," I said.

"It's going to be a long night," he said. "The tenants of these upper floors, they'll have to be questioned."

"You'll find them down in the club," I said. "I believe they're all at my private table with the producer and some of the network executives, entertaining them, I hope."

Sweeney told one of his men to empty the dead man's pockets, and as each item appeared Sweeney examined it —a comb, some loose change, a handkerchief smelling of patchouli, a gold cigarette lighter, no cigarettes or cigars . . . A real Hawkshaw he was, Lieutenant Al Sweeney, nose like a hound's.

"Who was this guy?" he said. "Somebody lifted his ID. Same reason somebody took the knife out of him."

"Or he didn't carry any identification," I said.

"Yeah. There's that." Sweeney walked around the corpse, seeming to study it. Suddenly he said, "Did you notice anything unusual about the knife?"

A detective's ploy. Catch the suspect off guard. But how could I be a suspect? I put it down to paranoia. Suspected of what? Of withholding evidence, maybe. I hoped I wasn't underestimating Detective Lieutenant Sweeney.

"It was a big knife," I said. "It had a two-edged blade.

23

I'm afraid I wasn't very observant, Lieutenant. I had all I could do, handling this fellow."

"In extreme situations very few persons are observant," Sweeney said. "They see only what's needed for survival. They'll tell you a story, though, when they've had time to think one up. The Russian police have a saying: He lies like an eyewitness." He laughed modestly. I managed a chuckle. "Well," he said, "maybe we'll luck out with some prints this time. Did you notice, was the other man wearing gloves?"

"I don't think so."

Sweeney walked around the apartment, chewing his bushy red moustache and scowling. Presently he came back to me.

"There's damned little to go on," he said. "Except this man's prints. I don't hope for much from ballistics."

Dom came in then. He merely glanced at the corpse and the torn-up apartment. Didn't flicker an eyelash. Domenico Ambrosini was the coolest maître d' of all time, though he looked more like the caricature of an undertaker. When he personally attended to a *flambé* he looked like a mortician dressing a corpse. He was tall and thin to the point of emaciation, with a cadaverous face, long bony hands, large dark tragic eyes. His voice came from somewhere deep in a dungeon. I'd swear it had an echo in it. I inherited him from my late partner, or more correctly, from my ex-partner's Uncle Rocco, *requiescat in pace.*

Dom said, "Sir?" He waited three beats, then said, "There's a phone call for you down at the bar, Mr. Streeter."

It had to be urgent. He wouldn't bring me a routine call. I asked Sweeney if he minded my leaving for a few minutes.

"Take care of business," he said.

I told Dom I'd be right down, and he bowed and left. It was not the bow of a hired man but the bow of a maestro who has just conducted Mahler's Eighth with four hundred voices and a thousand-piece orchestra. I often wondered about his home life, but I never knew. He disappeared when we closed in the morning and reappeared in the early evening, and he never engaged in personal talk. I liked to imagine him at his own table, surrounded by sons and daughters and grandchildren, with his fat and happy wife heaping more *saltimbocca* on his plate. But life being what it is, he probably lived in a furnished room and spent his lonely hours listening to old Caruso records.

As I started to follow him, Sweeney said, "I'll go with you." I waited. He spoke to his men. "I want prints of the dead man before anything else. Get them checked out to-night. Tell the medical examiner I want the slug out of the body for a ballistics report tonight. Repeat: Tonight. Let the bullets in the bedroom wall wait. Those came from Mr. Streeter's gun." To me he said, "I'm ready."

Sweeney gave a good performance. He spoke with accustomed authority. Direct, staccato speech. He acted as if he were in complete and perfect control. I wondered if he really thought he was. On our way downstairs we met an assistant medical examiner. Sweeney stopped him and told him about the knife, how it happened to be missing.

"So you shouldn't think some dumb detective took it prematurely," he explained. "Now, you'll also find a bullet in the decedent's back, and I'd like it out right away so my men can get to work on it. I want it before you do anything else, Doctor."

The medical examiner was a young man with the corn-fed look of an FBI agent, short hair, smooth face, blank stare.

"Thank you, Lieutenant," he said pleasantly. "We'll let you know."

Sweeney watched him go up the stairs. A couple of morgue attendants followed the examiner.

"He'll let me know," said Sweeney. "Twenty-five years in Homicide, and he'll let me know. Streeter, you have no idea what's happened in police work. The precinct detective's day is over. If the downtown boys don't take your case away from you . . . They'll be coming along any time now, Streeter, and when they do, I'd like to ask your cooperation with *me,* personally. They'll come because it's a burglary-homicide in a well-known nightclub, and they can get their mugs in the tabloids. So when they come, Streeter . . ."

"Understood," I told him. "Anything I can do."

Some detectives were coming up the stairs. Sweeney knew them from the burglary squad. He briefed them. We hurried on down.

There were more detectives and uniformed cops in the club, and because of them the place was still jammed with people long after the last show. They were getting some real, live drama. I told Sweeney to have a drink at the bar while I took my phone call.

As I made my way through the crowd, Bubba Antrim headed me off. He was the nightlife columnist for the last of New York's great tabloids. He was a walking encyclopedia of both high and low society, for they are frequently the same, and he knew where all the bodies were buried. He liked me and my jazz and Pal Joey's. He had reason, for the club had always been good copy. He put his hand on my arm.

"What's happening, Joey?"

He was a wispy, epicene little fellow, a dapper dresser, and well liked by most people, though hated by some. Knowledge isn't necessarily power, but it can be, and Bubba Antrim was a man of power.

I said, "I surprised a burglar upstairs."

"What's Homicide doing here?"

"I had to kill the burglar."

"Tell me about it."

26

"Wish I could, Bubba. Right now you know as much as I do."

"Great show tonight," he said. "I'm giving it a rave. May I call you tomorrow?"

"Please do. How'd you like Alice?"

"Marvelous! She's really the star of your show, you know. By the way, I don't see her with the others . . ."

He was looking toward my private table, where Heinz Morgenlicht and the studio execs were being entertained by the performers.

"She ducked out right after the show," I said. "A small *crise de nerfs,* you know, first-night jitters. Call me in the late morning."

I finally got to the phone. When I picked it up, it was banging and clanging like an old-fashioned cash register. My caller was dropping another coin, and Ma Bell in her dulcet tones was saying thanks.

When the line cleared I said, "Sorry to keep you waiting. This is Joseph Streeter."

A woman said, "Is it cool to talk, lover?"

For a second or two I didn't recognize the voice. Or rather, I did. Marilyn Monroe. I looked for Sweeney. He was hovering near.

"If you'd like to set up an appointment," I said, "perhaps we could . . ."

"How's the house, Joey?"

"The house?"

"Is it still crowded?"

"It's SRO."

"How'd they like me?"

"I can't talk business now," I told her. "Give me your number, I'll call you back."

She laughed that once famous Monroe laugh, a deep, soft, sexy, slightly psycho sound. Then she hung up. Sweeney moved in closer.

27

"Everything all right?"

"Actor's agent," I said. "Pushy type."

He looked skeptical. But it was his normal way of looking. The habit of detection. I thought he probably looked that way when he kissed his wife. If he was wondering why I had volunteered information above and beyond the call of duty, he said nothing about it. I didn't have to tell him it was an actor's agent, or comment that the agent was a pushy type. I didn't have to tell him anything. But I was still nervous from the fight upstairs, and I was doubly nervous now that Alice had called. Her mysteriously playful mood would have unnerved me if nothing else had.

Sweeney said, "Now I'd like to talk to the people who live on the upper floors, particularly the rear apartments."

Presumably he was thinking of the fire escape. Alice and Junep had those apartments. I took him to my table in the back corner. The performers were still in costume and makeup. Stacy Brown, my jazz singer, was on Heinz Morgenlicht's right, giving him the business. She was a big, bedluscious black mama, and she was wearing a slinky black satin gown with a plunging front, and Morgenlicht looked like he was about to take the plunge. On the producer's left, Colleen Costello, our all-purpose dancer (classical ballet, tap, soft-shoe, flamenco, Irish clog), a black-haired, blue-eyed beauty, was laying the blarney on with a trowel. Morgenlicht didn't seem to know which way to turn. I could have told him it didn't matter, for neither girl was about to turn anything for him. They had each other. Herb Junep and Doctor Caligari were also present. When I'd introduced Lieutenant Sweeney to everybody, Morgenlicht asked me about Alice, so I repeated my story about her being on the way to Atlantic City with a case of opening-night nerves.

Heinz Morgenlicht was a beefy, florid man, hairless as a

28

cue ball, with an outrageous reputation among young actresses. And, it was whispered, young actors.

"That switch ending," he said, *"The Cabinet of Doctor Caligari?* I like it. Keep it in."

"Thanks," I said.

"When will Alice return?"

"Thursday, for rehearsals."

"Have her call my office."

I said I would. Why should I say I wouldn't? Men in his position, some of them, will try to turn every business connection into a procurer. I don't even pimp for close friends. But why tell Morgenlicht? Let him find out for himself.

"Whose idea was that switch ending?" he asked. I told him it was Alice's. "The girl's a genius," he said. "You should pay her more money."

Caligari was looking at me with bitterness in his eyes. I'd stolen his thunder and given it to Alice. Had to. If I'd told Morgenlicht that Caligari thought up the switch, the producer might have asked him how or why, and I couldn't trust the magician to lie for me.

I excused myself on the pretext of having to see my maître d', and in fact I'd observed a little trouble at the street door, but as Dom wasn't on the floor at the moment I thought I'd better take care. Matt was blocking the doorway, preventing a blond floozie from entering. She was giving him hell. Loud and vulgar, still she was gorgeous. She wore a blond Afro wig, huge mirrored sunglasses, a shoulderless mid-thigh gold lamé sheath that fit her closer than a second skin, and four-inch red stiletto heels. She was chewing gum like a teenybopper and yammering about how she was by Christ coming in this goddamn joint, it was a goddamn public saloon, wasn't it? If she hadn't been carrying that outsize snakeskin handbag I gave her, I'd have taken her for one of our wilder Times Square hookers.

As I was leaving the table, Sweeney said, "I'll be wanting to talk to you later, Mr. Streeter."

I told him he'd find me up front. I went directly to the street door. You could hear Alice all over the room. She was doing a deep Brooklyn accent, blaring like a foghorn. Well, what *does* it sound like? Try sawing catgut with an unresined bow.

I rushed up to her, exclaiming, "Harriet! What kept you so long?"

"I got waylaid," she said, popping her bubble gum.

"Harriet, honey," I said, "I expected you an hour ago. It's nearly two-thirty."

This was not for Matt. He was cool, of course, but there were cops all over the place. Some were standing within earshot. Matt was staring at Alice, at this Times Square hooker, not sure of what he was seeing. Or hearing. Renée Taylor couldn't have done it better. Though I couldn't see Alice's eyes behind the big mirrored sunglasses, I knew she was laughing inside.

Matt said, "I'm sorry, boss. Sorry, Miss Harriet. I didn't . . . Hey! You're . . . !"

"Hold it," I told him. "Deaf-and-dumb."

"Got it," he said. "D-and-D it is. But you sure had me fooled, Miss—ah—otherwise I would've let you right in. Oh-oh! Boss, don't look now, but here comes that red-headed detective."

I waited until Sweeney came up behind me and spoke.

"Introduce me to this young lady, Streeter."

If Alice were worried, she didn't show it behind the mirrored glasses. She just smiled at Sweeney and went on poping her bubble gum.

"I'd like you to meet a very dear friend of mine, Lieutenant," I said. "This is Miss Harriet Maxwell." She did a little wiggle for him. "Harriet, this is Lieutenant Al Sweeney of Homicide."

Alice popped her bubble gum and said, "Howdja do, Lieutenant?"

"I'm pleased to make your acquaintance, Miss Maxwell," he said, charming as an Irish horse trader. "Do you perform here?"

She stopped chewing, turned the twin mirrors full on him, pursed her pretty lips, and purred, "Whadja have in mind, Lieutenant?"

She blew a bubble, a big one, and burst it with a loud pop. Sweeney's naturally pink face reddened. She slurped the gum back into her mouth and grinned at him. She'd got his Irish up, so he wouldn't be thinking clearly now. His neck swelled with the sudden rise in blood pressure. I could see him swallowing cotton, but he said nothing. He just stared at her like a cat watching a bird. She was a shrewd one, my Alice, and only nineteen.

She said, "So what we waitin' for, Joey? You buyin' or cryin'? Do I get a drink first, or do we go straight upstairs like last time?"

I said, "Sure, Harriet. Take a stool at the bar. I'll be right over."

As she turned to leave us she flung Sweeney a sexy smile and said, " 'Bye, Lieutenant."

She sashayed toward the back end of the bar, swinging her tail like Eve with an apple in her mouth looking for Adam. I hadn't seen that kind of walking since the old days on the Prado in Havana. Watching her walk, Sweeney's face got even redder. The mating look was in his eye, and himself a family man too.

Jimmy Joyce, my head barman, saw Alice coming and looked around for Dom, for of course he hadn't recognized her as a Times Square hooker. I caught his eye and gave him the office: Okay for this broad. He made room for her at the bar. We don't roust hookers at Pal Joey's if they're cool.

Alice didn't look too cool at the moment, but in fact she was. Sweeney had seen her only in her impersonations, or possibly as Alice the cigarette girl, if he'd seen her at all before this. He'd said he caught some of the show on television, but he hadn't said which parts. In any event, he'd never seen her as Harriet Maxwell.

"I'm surprised at you, Streeter," he said. I've described this harp as a gentleman, and of course a gentleman is by definition never unintentionally rude, so the feisty little mick was baiting me. "I remember that nice girl you were seeing last year," he blathered on, "that pretty ballerina from Chicago . . ."

"She was last year," I snapped. "Besides, she defected to the Bolshoi."

"All right," he said. "All right! But a hooker? Come *on*, Streeter! Since when do nightclub owners have recourse to prostitutes?"

"Are we throwing stones, Lieutenant?"

"I used to see you sometimes at Actors Chapel."

"You've been there lately?"

"Well, I hope you don't let her work your bar. You could lose your license, you know."

"Ease off, Lieutenant."

"Well, she's none of my business, unless she murders somebody. I never worked the vice squad."

"Tough. You could have retired rich, and we wouldn't have the present pleasure of your company. Now make yourself at home. Whatever you want is on the house. If I'm not here at the bar, you'll find me upstairs, in my apartment with Miss Maxwell."

He clenched his jaws and ground his teeth. I offered him an expensive Brazilian panatela. He accepted, and I held the match for him. Lieutenant Aloysius Sweeney might not have been all the gentleman I'd thought, but he was sure as hell a righteous man and intolerant of sinners. Though

I was eager to get Alice upstairs, I waited. I could see that Sweeney had something weightier on his mind than my morals.

"I've been thinking about the bullet hole in the dead man's back," he said. He puffed on his panatela and inhaled a good lungful. "Where did you say the other burglar was when he fired at you and shot his partner?"

"In the kitchen," I said. "He ran in there from the living room when I opened the hall door and turned on the lights."

"Yes, I see," Sweeney said. "And you and the man with the knife were struggling in the living room, just inside the hall door, right?" I said that was right. "Well, Streeter," he continued, "apparently you didn't notice, but you can't see the hall door from the kitchen. So whoever fired that shot wasn't in the kitchen at the time, unless he had a piece that could shoot around corners." I nodded agreement. "However," he concluded, "you can see the hall door from the bedroom and from the bedroom window. So who was the third man?"

"Good deduction," I said. "I should have been more observant."

Sweeney puffed on his cigar, eyeing me dubiously. He turned and looked toward the back end of the bar, where Alice sat cross-legged, chewing her bubble gum and grinning at us.

"Another thing," Sweeney said. "Whoever shot the man upstairs could have shot you too. I'm wondering why he didn't."

"That's a real puzzler," I said. "Now, if you don't mind, Lieutenant, my lady friend is waiting."

3

I left him then. The answer to his questions, and mine, was
sitting at the bar waiting for me. When Alice saw me leave
Sweeney and start toward her, she uncrossed her legs and
faced me square. Perching her pretty behind on the edge
of the bar stool she let her left leg hang down to bare a truly
breathtaking thigh. And she gave me what my daddy, who
was a sporting man, used to call The Look. It was Eve
herself who learned it from a friendly serpent, and since
then the great ladies of history have been known for it,
most recently Dietrich and Monroe. No doubt Mata Hari
had it on command. Certainly Cleopatra had it for Mark
Anthony. She'd already hooked Julius Caesar with it. And
the Queen of Sheba bewitched wise old Solomon with it.
But Alice's Harriet had something they all lacked. Bubble
gum.

As I came up to her, she raised her face to be kissed, and
when I kissed her I nearly broke up, for she'd really laid it
on. Eyelashes like palm fronds. Long and green. She'd
painted her luscious lips a shocking pink. A beauty spot like

a shiny black sequin gleamed on her darling chin close to the kissable mouth. What a trollop. She made Andrea True and Georgina Spelvin look like Boy Scouts. As I kissed her, the fragrance of Tigresse came cloying through ancient memories of sweaty nights in the mosquito swamps of Florida with a jug of triple-distilled white mule and Mamie, a brainless blond bundle of fluff who smelled of Tigresse all over. About as subtle as raw musk.

In other words, Alice's art was perfect. Had she done the Maid of Orleans in all her stark virginity, she'd have smelled of frankincense and myrrh. As a fellow artist I admired her control, since my nerves hadn't steadied yet and my stomach had a swarm of butterflies in it trying to get out. Even Alice's drink was in character. What would a Times Square hooker from Brooklyn drink at a classy bar? Tequila Sunrise. Through a straw. While slowly masticating bubble gum.

Jimmy Joyce poured a cognac for me. I knocked it back like a slug of red-eye and put the glass down. He refilled it. I let it sit while the first two ounces burned their way toward the butterflies. Jimmy could have gone about his business then, but he stood holding the bottle and looking quizzically at me. Jimmy Joyce was a bartender of the old school, the kind who polish glasses, an all but lost art. He was a small, wizened old man, but alert as a bird. Born in 1903 in Dublin of a publican father and a barmaid mother, Jimmy had toiled behind the stick since he was ten years old working in his parents' pub. At age sixteen, shortly before the Easter Rising, he fled Ireland with a price on his head for bombing and utterly destroying a British arsenal. When I found him he'd been working behind the same bar since he arrived in New York. In the years before Prohibition it was variously O'Toole's Bar & Grill, The Shannon, and The Cruiskeen Lawn. During Prohibition it went through several names and owners but always with Jimmy Joyce behind the stick. It was called O'Shea's Chop House and Clam Bar when I found it, and since I know a good barman when I see one, I kept him. Strange man. If ever a face had the haunted look, it was Jimmy's. He'd frankly admit it was because of the families of those British soldiers he killed when he bombed the arsenal. Remorse? No, he just figured someday one of the dead men's relations would walk in the street door and blow him away, for that, he declared, was what he'd do himself, bedad, if the shoe was on the other foot. Every new face across the bar belonged to a potential assassin. Jimmy Joyce waited stoically night after night for his executioner.

But now the haunted look was gone. Mischief danced like tiny stars in his eyes. He leaned across the bar, crooking a finger at me. I leaned closer. Alice cozied up to both of us. We must have looked like some kind of conspiracy. I glanced around for Sweeney and spotted him at my table with Morgenlicht and the others.

"It took a while," Jimmy whispered. "But I made her." Hearing this, Alice popped her bubble gum and pulled out of the conspiracy. She settled back in her bar seat and ignored us. Sotto voce, Jimmy said, "Know what tipped me, Joe?" He leaned closer. Alice stopped her chewing, ignoring us even harder. "Her *built!*" he said hoarsely. "Her *built!* There's no body like that body!"

Old men have their prerogatives, of course, so I merely stepped on his line.

"Except for her built," I told him, "she's incognito, and I want her to stay that way until I get a handle on what's happening."

"Dom told me about the burglar," he said. "You killed the guy?"

"Tell Dom for me, I want him to close up as soon as the television people have left. We'll stay dark tomorrow *and*

36

the Fourth. Time off with pay for everybody. Cleaners get double time. Tell Dom."

"It's true, then, you shot a burglar in Alice's apartment?"

He was looking at Alice as he spoke. She wasn't reacting. Or she was. She crossed her legs, swung one foot, popped her bubble gum, and stared happily around the room.

"Knifed," I said.

As I watched Alice sitting on her bar stool and carrying on, I remembered a low-life bar in Panama, the Copa de Oro, where I played piano when I was very young. The girls in that saloon turned tricks while sitting right at the bar, on the bar stools, damndest thing I ever saw. Watching Alice now, remembering that wild scene at the Copa de Oro, my vibes must have been visible, probably shocking pink like her lips, for she turned and saw the look in my eye, and she swung off her bar stool and grabbed my elbow.

"Hey, Joey!" she yelled, loud enough for everybody in the joint to hear. "We gonna get it on, or ain't we?"

"We'll be in my apartment," I told Jimmy.

He reached under the bar and pressed a button, unlocking the door that led to the inner stairway, a security measure dating from the time when we had card rooms on the parlor floor. I followed Alice through the doorway. There were still cops coming and going on the stairs and lower landings, but they didn't bother us. Presumably they knew who I was, and they must have thought they had my Times Square hooker figured too. Climbing the stairs behind Alice, my thoughts naturally turned to her reasons for the disguise, the skin-tight, shoulderless gold lamé sheath the blond Afro wig the harlot's makeup, and I reasoned that she must have been trying to avoid Charles and the fat Roman, meaning she knew they were after her. So they caught her anyway, despite the disguise, and they got the keys to her apartment. I'd heard Charles say that she'd spiked his instep with her stiletto heels, an old trick with ladies of the evening when confronted by difficult men. Where had she learned so much in her nineteen years? So she'd escaped, but here she was again. As for the fat Roman, or the third man, who'd shot Charles from the bedroom or the bedroom window, they could still be around and probably would be. And I hadn't a clue to the identity of either man. Well, no, I did have one clue: Alice. She could at least tell me why they'd burgled her apartment. Or rather, what they'd been looking for. I couldn't question her at the moment, since lawmen were everywhere within earshot.

By the time I'd triple-locked my hall door, I'd decided that since Alice had obviously not leveled with me I ought to try to proceed circumspectly. Questions may get answers, but they also give information. I assumed that she'd not been in legal possession of the dagger and the ring. Elementary. Well, all right, I don't cop moralistic attitudes about property, except when it comes to robbing the poor, but poor folks don't own antique jeweled daggers and ornate ruby rings. I needed answers from Alice, partly in order to try and protect her against the police and creeps like the late Charles's fat accomplice, and possibly a third man, but also to protect her interest in whatever the burglars had been after and failed to find.

It happens I like jewels for sentimental reasons. It was a bagful of Brazilian diamonds that enabled me to create Pal Joey's, so I'm grateful to the lovely little rocks. I worked hard for them against heavy opposition from Amazon River police patrols, a gang of *cangaçeiros*, the treachery of my own partners, and the jungle fever that turned my hair white. I still keep a few yellows and blue-whites in memory of that Amazon scam. So, if Alice needed my help, self-interest urged me on.

As soon as we were inside the apartment she went to the living room bar. Apparently the strain was telling, for she wasn't a drinker. Unlike most show people she didn't use anything at all, neither booze, grass, nor coke. Now she poured two cognacs, doubles, handed me one, and downed the other as I had done earlier in the club. Knocked it back like a longshoreman. I expected disaster, but she didn't bat an eyelash, didn't gasp, didn't even hiccough. She just took a deep breath and stared at me with those big Spanish eyes, motionless as a statue. Then with a deep shudder she exhaled.

"I'm going to revert to type, darling," she said, giving me The Look again and a small, snappy pop of her bubble gum. "Come, watch."

Still acting, but less Brooklyn now. As I followed her into the bedroom I wondered about that Brooklyn accent. Where could she have picked it up? In fact, you can't just pick it up. The pure Brooklynese twang-and-drawl is a complex and many-splendored thing, very difficult to simulate. But then I reminded myself that some performers don't have to learn. It's as if they've always known how, natural talents like the great Italian-American coloratura, Amelita Galli-Curci, or the Barrymores.

Alice switched on the lights of the dressing table that I'd installed in a corner for occasional ladies. She dropped her big snakeskin handbag on the floor, stepped out of her shoes, and sat before the mirrors. She peeled off the long green eyelashes and the blond Afro wig, letting her heavy chestnut hair fall to her shoulders. She picked up a brush and swept the hair back from her face, then dipped her fingers into a jar of cold cream and smeared two handfuls on the makeup, rubbing hard where she'd put mascara, rouge, and green eyeshadow. She wiped the cream away with tissues and finished with a face towel.

While she worked, I watched her and studied what old Jimmy Joyce called her built. She had the natural hourglass figure not uncommon among Spanish women, narrow waist, round hips, ample bosom. If Helen of Troy had a face that launched a thousand ships and burned the topless towers of Ilium, Spanish Alice had a waist that armies would itch to get their hands around. I told myself to take care of business. Show time. For openers I went back to the beginning.

"Why did you crab Caligari's act? What made you duck out like that?"

She stood up and faced me, looking me straight in the eyes with the honest gaze of a used-car salesman, and said, "I had to go make wee-wee."

I slapped her good across the cheek. It staggered her. I grabbed her shoulders and held her steady.

"Don't kid around," I told her. "I had to kill a man tonight because of you. What were Charles and his fat friend looking for?"

She smiled up at me as if I'd kissed her. I raised an open hand. She closed her eyes and waited, still smiling. So I took her in my arms and held her close. Presently she looked up into my eyes, not smiling now. Hers were brimming with tears.

"They were after Carlota's Rosary," she whispered hoarsely. "It belonged to my mother. It's a family heirloom."

"Tell me about it."

"It's a rosary of pearls and amethysts, worth a hundred thousand dollars," she said. She put her arms around my neck and hung there. "That's just for the pearls and the amethysts," she explained. "The provenance of the Rosary makes it worth five times that much. Do you know about these things, Joey?"

"Tell me about the provenance."

"Well, Carlota's Rosary was handed down from my great-grandmother, who was lady-in-waiting to Empress Carlota Amalia, the wife of Maximilian the First of Mexico.

He was the brother of Franz Josef the First of Austria, and for this reason Napoleon the Third gave Mexico to the Hapsburgs and made Max the emperor. It was all comic opera, pure Strauss. Anyway, Empress Carlota gave the Rosary to my great-grandmother for safekeeping during their stay in Rome, where Carlota had gone to seek help for Maximilian, who was losing the Mexican War of Independence to Benito Juárez. No one in Europe would help poor Max, not his brother, Franz Josef, not even Napoleon, who had made him Emperor of Mexico. When even the Pope refused aid, Carlota went mad, literally insane, and of course she forgot that she'd given the Rosary to her lady-in-waiting. Its absence from the crown jewels wasn't noticed for many years, and by then Carlota couldn't give a clear account of it. My great-grandmother said nothing. In time she gave it to her daughter, my grandmother, and she gave it in turn to my mother. I didn't know we had it until I discovered Mamá's diary, after she died, six months ago."

She buried her face in my chest and wept, sobbing a little. I held her closer. After a while, I asked her how she knew the value of the Rosary, and presently she sniffled a little, sighed, and answered.

"When I came east I had it appraised at a jeweler's on Forty-seventh Street, and he said the pearls and amethysts alone are worth a hundred thousand dollars. Natural pearls are very hard to match exactly, not like cultured pearls. I didn't tell him the Rosary's provenance. According to Mamá's diary she had it appraised herself by a jewel designer she could trust, and he said its provenance made it worth half a million."

"So that's what the burglars were after," I said. "Where'd you hide it?"

She peeled off her dress and dropped it on the floor. Under it she'd been wearing neither bra nor panties, only

41

the Rosary looped once around her slender waist. The crucifix dangled in her heavy dark pubic hairs.

I knelt so I could examine the pearls more closely. The five decades of Ave Marias were very large, perfectly matched pearls of high luster. The Glorias and paternosters were amethyst beads even larger than the pearls. The chain and the cross were gold, the Christ silver. He glowed in the curly dark bush where He hung. Alice must have put some Tigresse there. It was very heavy.

While I examined the Rosary, marveling at the rich sheen of the pearls, I asked her to tell me also about the dagger. She didn't ask how I knew about the dagger. Instead she answered the question.

"It's also an heirloom," she said. "It belonged to Emperor Maximilian. Come up here, Joey."

I stood up and took her in my arms again. She clasped her fingers behind my neck and leaned back. I pulled her up close and nuzzled her neck.

"Tell me about it," I said.

"Max wore it when he faced the firing squad," she said. "Benito Juárez had him shot." She ran her left leg between mine, and pressed. She said, "There's a motto etched into both sides of the blade: *Seré cadáver pero no gusano.* It means, 'I shall be a cadaver, but not a worm.' "

"And did Empress Carlota Amalia give it to her lady-in-waiting, your great-grandmother, for safekeeping, like the Rosary?" She breathed a soft yes in my ear. I cupped her cheeks in my hands and pulled her hips hard against me. "So the dagger's an heirloom too," I said. "And the ruby ring?"

"Yes."

She was working on my fly now. I pulled off my jacket and flung it on a chair. She had my belt undone.

"How did the burglars know you had these things?"

"One of them was Mamá's consort."

42

"Charles?"

I was getting out of my shirt. She was pulling down my pants and shorts.

"You said *was* your mother's consort?"

"Yes. She kicked him out not long before she died."

She was taking off my socks.

"Tell me about Charles's fat friend."

"Who?"

She stood up and pressed herself against me, and I was losing interest in questions. I wanted answers, but not the kind these questions were getting.

I said, "There was a fat man with Charles. He got away."

"I don't know."

"Is Charles the reason you didn't finish the act with Caligari?"

She didn't answer. She was doing something more to the point. I tried to press a different point. I told her I had it figured, she'd seen Charles in the audience during the show, and that's why she disappeared. She pulled away from me and went to the bed and lay down on her back, watching me but saying nothing. I stood where she'd left me, waiting for an answer.

"You're right," she said coolly. "I saw Charles and I panicked. I knew what he was after. When I went down through the trapdoor that last time, I did a quick change with some things I found in the wardrobe. Then I went out through the garden and the alleyway. Charles was always very clever. He and the fat man you mentioned were waiting for me in the alley. The fat one had a gun. They took my key case, but I got away."

"Where did you go?"

"I walked, just walked. I didn't know what to do."

"Why didn't you call the police?"

"Because I don't know if the Rosary really belongs to me, Joey. It's been in my family for three generations, but le-

43

gally it may still belong to Carlota's family, the Belgian royal house, or to Maximilian's family, the Hapsburgs, or to the Mexican government. Joey, none of them would ever miss it, not now, not after all this time, and they don't need it. I do."

"Oh, I agree," I said. "But you could have told me all this before it came to burglary. I had to kill a man."

"I'm sorry, Joey. It's just that I didn't want to get you involved. And I didn't think Charles would follow me all the way to New York. How do you suppose he found me, anyway?"

"You've been in *Variety* and the other papers, honey. If he knew you were into theater . . ."

"Oh, of course, he knew I went to UCLA. He knew I was in dramatics there. So I guess he sort of figured . . . Anyway, he didn't get Carlota's Rosary. It's *ours* now, Joey. We can split a cool half million."

"We'd be lucky to get ten percent," I told her.

"Well, that's fifty thou, isn't it? We could buy a Rolls Royce."

She was being kittenish, lying there on the bed, flat on her back, doing her Marilyn Monroe.

I said, "You couldn't buy half a Rolls for fifty. And I meant ten percent of a hundred thousand, not half a million. Try to sell the Rosary with its true provenance and the Hapsburgs would get you for sure, if they haven't all died of hemophilia. Peddle the Rosary just for the pearls and amethysts, you're lucky if you clear ten grand."

"But there must be somebody who'll pay us what it's worth, Joey."

"I could ask around."

"Oh, Joey! Would you?"

"For you," I said. "Anything."

4

Fire trucks' bells and heavy mortar fire reached me through dense fog. I tried to listen. Screw it, I thought, let the city burn. Alice suddenly sat up. My foxhole buddy. I threw an arm over her to pull her down again.

"Joey!" she whispered. "Somebody's at the door!"

"Who cares? Come back to sleep."

The ringing and banging started up again.

"For God's sake, Joey! See who it is, will you?"

I unstuck my eyelids and rolled out of bed and put on a robe. The nightstand clock said six A.M. An aerial bomb shook the building like one of those mini-quakes you get in San Francisco. Kids of all ages just can't wait for the Fourth.

Lieutenant Aloysius Sweeney waited at the door, looking haggard, with bags like Gladstones under his eyes.

In a voice thin with fatigue he said, "Sorry to wake you, Streeter, but I have a few questions."

"Come in," I said. "You look like I feel. I'll brew up some strong coffee."

"That's the last thing I need, Streeter. I've been swilling

45

coffee by the quart in the club kitchen. If you want to do something for me, let me have a quiet drink."

"You've got it. Come along." I led him to the bar and went behind it. "What's your pleasure, Lieutenant?"

"A boilermaker, if you don't mind."

"Call your shot."

"Bourbon, please."

I gave him a triple Jack Daniel's in a highball glass and a schooner of Harp. To make him feel at ease I had the same. While I poured the shots and drew the beers, he leaned heavily against the bar. His naturally pink face was almost white with fatigue.

"You should be home in bed," I told him. "You're no younger than I, and I'm dead tired."

"Streeter," he said, raising his glass, "you're a prince." We drank to that. He downed the triple in one long swallow, took a pull at the schooner of beer, wiped the foam off his moustache, and straightened up, a rejuvenated man. His color was back. His eyes were bright. "Streeter," he said, "I'm remembering what happened here a year ago, when your partner was murdered. If it hadn't been for you, my investigation would have gone much differently. I could have made a live collar."

"That's gratitude," I said. I'd drunk only half my drink, but already I was feeling mellow. "If it hadn't been for me," I said, "you wouldn't have made a collar at all, dead or alive. And here you come complaining a whole year later. You got your lieutenancy out of it. Isn't that enough for you?"

"That it is," he said. "I'm a humble man, Streeter. But I would dearly love to make a live collar this time."

"I hope you do. Tell me though, Lieutenant, isn't this case really for Safe and Loft? It's just a burglary. I mean, what I did was self-defense. This isn't a murder case."

"Ah, but it is," said Sweeney. He pulled some folded

46

papers out of an inside coat pocket and unfolded them on the bar. Computer printouts. "I'll just summarize," he said. "First, those three bullets in the living room wall upstairs came from a twenty-five caliber automatic of unknown make and registry, probably European. We found the ejected shells, too, but they don't help. We do better with the bullet fragments in the dead man's back. They came from a thirty-eight fired from a Colt 'Detective Special' that belonged to an off-duty Los Angeles cop who was shot and killed when he attempted to intercept a one-man bank robbery in Hollywood last January. The robber was described as a very tall man wearing sunglasses. He was wounded in the gunfight but got away. He took the dead cop's gun." Sweeney paused, shuffling the papers. "So you see," he said, "it has become a murder case."

I said, "Yes, I see."

"Now, the stiff you made," he said, "is very tall, or he would be if he could stand up." Sweeney smiled, pleased with his jest. "The bank robber was also very tall. Do you consider coincidences, Streeter?"

"I'm not the philosophical type," I said. "But congratulations. I see what you mean. It's a murder case, all right, and it looks like you've got one up on the LAPD. Collared a cop killer."

"Don't make jokes," he said. "Listen to this. Charles Louis Urquhart, born Nineteen thirty-two, Denver, no police record in this country but known to Interpol as an international playboy, swindler, and jewel thief, arrested in five European countries, never convicted but deported each time. Last December he was the escort of the Principessa Francesca di Casoli on the evening she was robbed, raped, and murdered in her Beverly Hills home. He never gave any testimony but his original statement, which was to the effect that he and the principessa were accosted by a man with a gun, forced to let him into her home, where he had her tie up her escort, then raped her, forced her to open the safe, stole her jewels, raped her again, and then strangled her with a length of telephone cord. Urquhart was held as a material witness, but despite his shady European record he was eventually released. He said the perpetrator was a black man of average height and build, probably in his late twenties, bearded, wearing a brown suit, no hat, spoke with a southern accent. Do you smell a black herring, Streeter?"

"Distinctly, Lieutenant."

"So what I need to know is what those burglars were looking for, and did they find it in Miss Los Angeles . . . How do you pronounce her name, Streeter?"

"María de los Ángeles Farah Gómez. Call her Alice. It's her stage name."

"What were they looking for in her apartment?"

"I don't follow," I said.

My daddy used to say a lie is best built on a strong foundation. Build it on a small truth. If I didn't follow Sweeney, it's because I was way ahead of him. I certainly would not impede an investigation into a cop killing. Indeed, I intended to do whatever I could to help Sweeney in that direction. But first things first. I also intended to protect Alice and her interest, now *our* interest, in Carlota's Rosary.

"Let me explain," Sweeney said. "This Charles Louis Urquhart was an unconvicted jewel thief. He was on the scene at a Beverly Hills jewel robbery. He gets killed with a dead cop's gun . . ."

"I thought *I* killed him," I said.

"It's a toss-up. The bullet did a lot of damage including a big fragment in the heart. The knife tore him up inside. He was a dead man either way. But what I need to know is this: Did Alice have any jewelry?"

"Oh, I doubt it," I said. "Poor but honest, and very

young. Given time, with her looks and talent, she'll have diamonds as big as the Ritz. Right now, Lieutenant, she's got nothing but great expectations."

"I also need to know," he said, "who was the third man. He shot Urquhart in the back. He used a murdered cop's gun. So our third man could be the bank robber, the cop killer. Then why didn't he shoot *you* while he was shooting Urquhart? If he could see you two fighting over the knife, he could have seen you well enough to hit you at that range. I think he meant to kill Urquhart and had no reason to shoot you too, unless he thought you'd seen him. He would have been hard to see, on the fire escape outside the bedroom window. You're a lucky man."

"You need a little luck," I said.

"If that thirty-eight slug hadn't been a hollow-point," Sweeney said, "it could have gone right through Urquhart and killed you too. You've got the luck of the Irish. Pity you're not." He waited for a reaction. I let him wait. "Well," he said, "what do you think?"

"About what, Lieutenant?"

"All this. It adds up to something."

"Beats me," I said. And it was true. "I'm not too sharp this morning. Less than three hours' sleep, you know. Let me get a little shut-eye, we can talk later in the day."

Sweeney looked deep into his whiskey glass as he murmured, "Miss Maxwell stay over?"

"She's still sleeping. I wish I were."

"One more question," he said. I thought, here it comes, the big one. I topped off his whiskey glass and drew him a fresh beer. He said, "How come you didn't tell me your doorman lives in the basement?"

"Go home," I told him. "Go to bed, Lieutenant. You're overtired. So am I."

"But how come you didn't tell me?"

"Because at the time we were discussing the people who

49

live on the *upper* floors, Lieutenant. The burglary took place on the third floor, not down in the basement."

"Now don't get your balls in an uproar," he said. "I was just asking how come your doorman lives in the basement . . ."

"That's not what you were asking at all," I said. "You were asking why I hadn't told you Matt Griffin lives in the basement, not how come he lives there."

"All right, then, I'm asking."

I explained that Matt's room had been the office, but nowadays I used a CPA service. I moved the antique iron safe and the rolltop desk up to my apartment and kept cash and records there. Since Matt was a highly sociable old man and liked having a lot of people around, and since his bedroom, the former office, was just off the greenroom, he got a lot of traffic. There was a complete bath down there for the performers, so he used it too. And he ate in the club's kitchen.

"Where was he last night around the time of the incident upstairs?" Sweeney asked.

"At the street door," I said.

"How would you know that? You were upstairs."

"Well, where in hell *would* he be, for God's sake?"

"Just take it easy, Streeter." He consulted one of his computer printouts. "One thing about these new procedures," he said, "the computers can get you any kind of information on anyone you're interested in. For instance, I know that your Matthew Mark Griffin has a license to carry a Model Nineteen-aught-eight 'Luger' Naval Parabellum. A war souvenir. I also know that your comic, Herbert Edward Junep, did time in Nevada for hotel theft. Your singer, Stacy Brown, has a brother in Attica for armed robbery. Your headwaiter, Domenico Ambrosini, has a record in Italy, some kind of political activity. Your head bartender,

James Joseph Joyce, is suspected of raising money for the IRA . . ."

"All right," I said. "You've made your point. The NYPD sees all, knows all . . ."

"How did you acquire the money to set up Pal Joey's?"

"Worked hard all my life, went without lunch, saved my pennies . . ."

"Well, it's a matter for the IRS, and no business of mine," he said. "Now, about the tenant of the apartment that was burgled, this Alice, we found her prints all over the place, naturally, and you gave me her name and her description, but when we put it all in the computer nothing came out. Not even Immigrations has a line on María Los Angeles . . . God damn it! Why can't I get her name right?" He looked at one of the printouts. "María de los Ángeles Farah Gómez," he said, mispronouncing it slowly and carefully. "So I had her double-checked under Farah and under Gómez, because of the backwards way these Spanish people write their names. Nothing, Streeter. If we can't get a line on a person, that person doesn't exist. This Alice is a figment of somebody's imagination unless you can give me more information. What do you know about her, where she really comes from . . . ?"

"You checked with Actors Equity?"

"First thing we did. She's Mexican, you said? Equity has her, but U.S. Immigrations never heard of her. What is she, some kind of a wetback?"

"She'll be here for rehearsals Thursday. You can talk to her yourself."

"So you said. If she should happen to get in touch meanwhile . . ."

"Of course," I said. "If she calls . . ."

"Thanks."

"Pleasure."

"Now, one more question, and I'm done," he said.

"What about that last-minute switch to the ending of the magic show? I picked up on your conversation with Morgenlicht. So I inquired about it later, after you left us. Tell me about it."

"It's true," I said. "Doctor Caligari had a brainstorm. I told Morgenlicht it was Alice's idea, but it was really Caligari's. It worked, so we're keeping it in."

"In an investigation we look for the unusual," Sweeney said. "Now, they also tell me that Caligari and the girl who disappears in the cabinet, Alice, didn't come back to take their bows."

"That's what made the ending effective," I said. "She goes into the cabinet and disappears. Then he goes in. The stagehands come and dismantle the cabinet and carry it off. The magician and the girl do not reappear. The illusion is complete."

"Come off it, man! I've been working Times Square a long time now, Streeter, many years, and I've known a lot of theater people. One thing's for sure, if you want to keep an actor from taking a bow, you have to break both legs and tie him down. Or her, as the case may be."

"It's been several questions," I said, "since you asked for just one more."

"Why do I get the feeling, Streeter, that you are not cooperating?"

"Have another drink, Lieutenant."

"No, thanks. I'll push on." He glanced at his wristwatch. "Seven o'clock," he said. "Before I go, could I have one of those cigars like the one you gave me last night?" I kept a box of Brazilians behind the bar. I offered it, and he took a few and stowed them away. He took one more, bit the end off it, and puffed as I held the match. "Good for cutting the smell of liquor," he said, "should a snoop from Internal Affairs happen to pass by."

Men have been shot for less.

5

When Sweeney left I went back to the bedroom with two things in mind. One was Sweeney's question about Alice's identity. But she wasn't there, so the other thing I had in mind was moot. I looked in the bathroom, of course, and on the mirror over the washstand she'd written with orange lipstick: "Back for dinner, love and kisses. María la Loca." Which means Mary the Mad, or Crazy María. So what else was new? Back for dinner, and it was only a little after seven A.M. I rubbed out the writing with a tissue, just in case Lieutenant Sweeney or another detective managed to get it.

Then I checked the guest bedroom and bath, the library, front parlor, dining room, kitchen and pantry. She could not have left by the hall door of the living room, for Sweeney and I were in there. The back door, leading to the porch and the garden stairs, was wired to ring chimes when opened. She knew about the chimes. So she'd left by the hall door of the guest bedroom. She was sneaking out. But why leave at all? She was safer if she stayed put. In any case, she'd left as herself, for the blond Afro wig and long green eyelashes were where she'd dropped them the night before. Of course, Carlota's Rosary was gone with her, no doubt wrapped around her slender waist.

I went back to the living room bar and washed the glasses while I tried to think, but I was too tired to think, and a little drunk, so I went into the kitchen and preared a pot of coffee. While it was dripping, I listened to the seven o'clock news. The announcer was just getting around to the local scene.

The events at Pal Joey's made up the lead story. It didn't include all the facts as Lieutenant Sweeney had just reported them to me, but it did include one detail not mentioned by him, namely, at the request of the NYPD the New Jersey State Police had put out a pickup-and-hold on María de los Ángeles Farah Gómez, also known as Alice, wanted for questioning in last night's burglary-homicide at Pal Joey's and believed to be vacationing in Atlantic City. Her description followed, just as I'd given it to Sweeney: ". . . nineteen years old, five feet four inches tall, one hundred twenty pounds, shoulder-length dark brown hair, dark brown eyes, light olive complexion." With that description you could pick up a few million young women before breakfast.

The boilermakers I'd drunk with Sweeney had stupefied me somewhat, but a cup of black coffee cleared my mind, as clear as it ever gets. I went into the bathroom and took a quick shave and shower, turning on the cold spray for one agonizing moment at the end, and after that I felt ready to fight a bear and eat him raw. I dressed, including the P-38, and went up to the third floor. There were no cops around now, but the NYPD had sealed Alice's apartment, as is customary when there's been a felony of sufficient weight, say a murder or a narcotics raid. I went down the hall to Caligari's and rang his bell. Not that I thought Alice would be there, but she had to be somewhere on the upper floors, it seemed to me, for she surely wouldn't go down to the club or out onto the street as herself. Caligari didn't answer his doorbell, so I used my master keys.

The smell of slivovitz was heavy in the living room. The place smelled like a Hell's Kitchen saloon at four A.M. I found the magician in his bedroom snoring like an asthmatic goat. An empty bottle lay on the floor by the bed.

I went through the rooms opening windows to air out the joint, and when I returned to the bedroom to wake Caligari, a small surprise shook me down to my shoes. I saw a familiar earring on the bedroom dresser. It was a cabochon opal pendant on a gold chain, and it looked like half of a pair I'd given Alice.

I dropped it in my pocket, then shook Caligari awake. I told him Alice was missing again.

"Again?" he mumbled. He raised up on one elbow, squinting like an albino. He looked horrible. Dracula with a slivovitz hangover. "She come back?"

"She did, and she's gone again. If you see her, grab her and keep her out of sight. Otherwise do nothing till you hear from me." He made a grumbling noise and fell back on the bed groaning. "And what in hell is one of her earrings doing on your dresser, John?"

"Earring?" he moaned. He belched hugely and looked like he might throw up. I fished the earring out of my pocket and dangled it close to his eyes. "Earring?" he said. "Earring? Don't remember."

Obviously a bad case of wet brain. I knew he drank, but I hadn't known he was a drunk. A very secretive and private man, John Radulovich, a/k/a Doctor Caligari.

"Go back to sleep," I told him.

I wanted to drive a stake through his heart. I went upstairs thinking about that goddamn earring. It certainly looked like the one I'd given to Alice. Assuming it was, I wondered what else to assume. She and Caligari worked together, so why shouldn't she be in his apartment at one time or another? As for her taking off her earrings in his bedroom . . . Probably she'd lost it, in the living room of course, and he'd found it and simply placed it on his bedroom dresser for safekeeping. Of course. Jealousy is like the taste of bile in the throat. I told myself I'd better clean up my act. Forty-nine years old and jealous of a teenager. Well, nineteen *is* one of the teens. It's also more like twenty-nine with some women. I told myself to forget the earring and try to concentrate on Carlota's Rosary. I did so, and it helped.

Having found one earring in Caligari's bedroom, I wasn't ready to find the other one in Herb Junep's apartment, so I tried the girls first, Stacy and Colleen. Also it seemed not unlikely that Alice had fled to their place if she'd been eavesdropping on my dialogue with Lieutenant Sweeney. She'd panicked and run to the girls.

Stacy answered the door wearing a man's pajama top. It was unbuttoned to the navel. Her fine brown frame was much like Alice's, except of course for color. She was cinnamon, and she hailed from New Orleans.

"Mornin', Joey," she said. "C'mon in. Have a cup of coffee." She had a smile that could light up Times Square at blackout time. I asked her if she'd seen Alice this morning. "She left about fifteen minutes ago, Joey. Said she was goin' to mass. You comin' in, honey?"

I followed her into the kitchen. Colleen was seated at the breakfast table having croissants and café au lait. The smell of chickory reminded me of my own time in New Orleans, playing piano at night in a Bourbon Street saloon, having coffee and doughnuts at the Café du Monde in Jackson Square early in the morning when the air was cool and fresh and you heard the horse carts and the songs of the peddlars. I was Alice's age then. Stacy poured me a large cup of the café au lait and I helped myself to the croissants. Anxiety and Jealousy fly out the windows when Hunger walks in the door. I even had eyes for Colleen. She was wearing the bottom half of Stacy's pajamas. Or vice versa. Colleen was a pretty girl and built along the slim, boyish lines of the dancer, small breasts, straight hips, slender neck. She had the clear white skin, dark blue eyes, and raven hair of those Irish whose ancestry has a castaway from the storm-wrecked Spanish Armada.

She and Stacy had a nice act. Stacy sang ballads and blues while I played accompaniment and Colleen danced the interpretation. They'd been doing this bit with pickup piano players in Long Island clubs for about a year when they came to Pal Joey's one weekday afternoon and I auditioned them. Stacy sang, "Bad-ass Stacy Brown, baddest ass in the whole damn town!" Colleen gave it a lazy shuffle and a slow grind. I hired them.

Colleen also did a solo, no accompaniment at all, a virtuoso number. Wearing the customary black tights, bolero jacket with starched shirt front, wing collar and tie, top hat, and walking stick, she danced routines using tap and acrobatics so difficult they didn't look possible. Hard to believe even as you watched her. With heels and toes, cane-tapping and finger-popping, she got rhythms going that crescendoed like a drum roll until she had the customers on their feet calling *Go! Go! Go!*

Funny about Colleen: Though there was passion in her dancing, I never saw any offstage. Here she was, sitting at the kitchen table naked from the waist up, cool as an ice cube, biting into a croissant and bidding me good morning as if she didn't have bare tits or I were not a man. True, they were quite small.

I asked where Alice had said she was going to mass, but Stacy said she hadn't mentioned which church.

57

"She just asked to borrow a change of clothes," Colleen spoke up. "Something wrong, Joe?"

"She's in trouble," I said. "I've got to find her and get her out of sight. There's a pickup-and-hold on her in connection with last night's burglary. The police want to question her. I don't want them to. Neither does she, so I don't understand why she's going to mass. She'll be seen. What's she wearing?"

"My white linen pants suit," Stacy said, "with red shoes and a red beret."

"Is she carrying that big snakeskin bag I gave her?"

"Yes."

"Would you girls help me find her? I'd like you to go to Actors Chapel and Saint Patrick's. They're the most likely in this neighborhood. You can split up, to make it faster."

Colleen said, "What kind of trouble could she be in, Joe? You killed the burglar, Alice didn't."

"Please," I said. "There's no time. Will you check out Saint Pat's and Actors Chapel?"

Stacy said, "Don't worry, Joey. We'll take care."

She walked me to the door, and before she unlocked it she gave me a big hug and a juicy kiss. If I'd closed my eyes I could have been holding and kissing Alice. It was a bit confusing to me in my present state, especially as Stacy gave me The Look à la Bourbon Street as I left.

I hurried down the hall to Herb Junep's apartment. He didn't answer his bell, so I let myself in with the master keys. I'd thought of sending him downtown to Our Lady of Guadalupe, on 14th Street, for Alice went there sometimes to hear mass in Spanish. But then I had an insane thought: What if she was *here?* I didn't really *think* she would be, only that she might, if you can call that thinking. The opal earring on Caligari's dresser (now in my pocket) indicated that there might be a side to Alice I hadn't suspected. And if Caligari, why not Junep? My thinking was about as rational as any middle-aged man's in the grip of a juvenile passion, and I knew it. I was very angry with myself and ready to kill one fat Roman burglar if I found him stalking her with his little .25-caliber automatic. I was ready to kill any man who came near her for whatever reason. I was fit to be tied.

As I let myself into the apartment I called out, "Hey, Herb! It's me, Joe."

He didn't answer. Junep frequently went out tomcatting and didn't get home till morning. Then he'd sleep till late afternoon. I went into the bedroom, but he wasn't there, though his bed had been slept in. One of the bedroom windows was open. I found him in the bathroom, naked in a full tub of steaming scarlet water, with a big hole in his midriff just below the rib cage, precisely where I'd stuck Charles Louis Urquhart. No question, it was a knife wound. And the knife was missing. My hands began to tremble. It was the coincidence, for Sweeney liked coincidences. He'd asked me if I believed in them. I'd evaded the question by saying I wasn't the philosophical type, but in fact I was fully aware of Jung's work on coincidence and before him Kammerer's Law of Seriality. The coincidence at hand would surely impress the lieutenant, as it would any police detective.

I noticed a shiny wet red place on the back of Junep's head. I reached under the water and found his wrist. No pulse. I felt his throat. No pulse there either. I lifted one of his eyelids. The pupil was wide and dark and showed no reaction when I passed my other hand before the eye. I wiped my hands on a towel. The scarlet water made a pink stain on the cloth.

I went through the apartment looking for a clue to the reason for his murder, but I didn't know what sort of clue I was looking for. I found no evidence of burglary, though there might have been something I overlooked or didn't recognize. I couldn't imagine what Junep might have had

59

that a burglar would want, but then I hadn't known that Alice had had anything of value, save her lovely self. Still, there seemed to be evidence that Junep's murder was a part of last night's affair, for the knife wound had clearly been made by a large, two-edged blade, and the knife was missing.

I decided not to call 911 right away, for three reasons: It wasn't my homicide, Junep could wait, and I needed to find Alice before I talked to cops.

It was odd about the bedroom windows. Though one was open, the other had an air-conditioner turned on high and cold. I thought about it, then went back to the hall door and locked it from the inside. I left the apartment by way of the open window and took the fire escape to the roof. I saw nobody up there, though there were some sunbathers atop a brownstone four buildings west. I checked the rooftop doorway. Locked. I went to the front of the roof and looked down. It was only eight o'clock Sunday morning, so naturally the street was empty. Except of course for Sweeney's city car and one blue-and-white. I crossed the roof and went down the ladders to my floor. My back porch overlooked the garden, and a stairway led down to it. The porch led into my back parlor.

There were windows on each side of the porch door, and one of them stood slightly raised, just a crack. I saw the mark of a jimmy on the wooden sill. The window catch had been snapped off.

6

Remembering last night's nearly fatal delay in shooting, I unlimbered the P-38 and released the safety before I unlocked the door. I intended to shoot first this time and think about it later. But in room after room I found no one, nor did I see any trace of a search. The window had been jimmied during the past hour, for I'd gone through the whole apartment looking for Alice only a few minutes after seven o'clock, when Sweeney left, and I would have noticed the window standing slightly open had it been jimmied earlier. I checked the hall doors. The main hall door was unlocked. So the intruder had entered by jimmying a rear window and then walked out the hall door. I had arrived possibly seconds later.

I holstered my gun, went to the kitchen cabinet where I kept my tools, got out a hammer and a handful of three-inch flathead nails, and nailed the jimmied window shut. Then I nailed the other one shut too. Why no window gates? Some people, in fact several millions of our fellow citizens, get that jailhouse feeling with bars over the win-

61

dows, and I'm one of them. Anyway, I always kept the P-38 handy, and I'd never had a burglary. Nor had I one now, apparently, for so far as I could tell, nothing but the window had been disturbed in any of the rooms. Nothing had been stolen. As for calling the police, if I wasn't going to report a homicide, I was certainly not about to call 911 on a mere breaking-and-entering.

Besides, I had a theory, and I felt sure that Lieutenant Sweeney would have the same: If the burglars hadn't found what they were looking for in Alice's apartment last night, they might have come looking for it in mine this morning, assuming they knew about our relationship.

I wished I'd questioned her further before taking her to bed. Or had *she* taken *me* to bed? But questioning her at all, what with her gorgeousness draped all over me, was a miracle of machismo. Lesser men would have failed utterly.

As for questions, I realized I had one for Sweeney. Doubtless I should have asked him earlier, when he woke me up, but I was groggy from lack of sleep, and the boilermakers didn't clarify my mind.

I found him in the club, sitting alone at my private table, writing in his notebook. A uniformed cop stood by the street door, another by the garden door. Otherwise the club was empty. It was dark except near the windows and at my table, where Sweeney had turned on an area light. It was quiet, and it still smelled from last night's booze and smoke and bodies. By nightfall the air-conditioners would freshen it up. An empty cabaret in the early morning is a lonely place. Like a haunted house. You still feel the presence of the people who belong there.

Sweeney looked haggard, but he seemed to have picked up energy. His manner was bright and alert.

As I came up to the table he said, "Couldn't sleep?"

"Been thinking," I told him. I sat across the table from

him. "I'm curious to know what was stolen in that rape-murder in Beverly Hills last December."

"You thinking it ties in?"

"No."

"Then what's your interest?"

"I'm not interested, just curious. Do you mind my asking?"

"Here's the computer printout of the list," he said, handing me a folded paper.

He watched me as I studied it. I was looking for something that could be hidden in a coffee can, or a sugar or flour container, such as those that had been dumped on Alice's kitchen floor. There were four items:

1. *Carlota's Rosary.* Five decades of matched white pearls, with amethyst Glorias and paternosters, chains and cross of gold, Christ of silver. Part of Empress Carlota's crown jewels. Value $500,000.

2. *Spanish Dagger.* Two-edged dirk of Toledo steel, 11-inch blade incised with motto: *Seré cadáver pero no gusano.* ("I shall be a cadaver, but not a worm.") Gold guard, ivory hilt studded with seven star sapphires, typical Spanish Notch in the choil. Presentation dagger from Napoleon III to Maximilian I of Mexico. Value $50,000.

3. *Lady's Ring.* Rose gold band, with pigeon-blood rubies set in platinum filigree, designed by Count Carlo. Value $10,000.

4. *Catherine's Egg.* Russian Easter Egg of cat's-eye (alexandrite) weighing 5,071 carats, wrapped in gold-wire net with emeralds at the interstices, mounted on a fire-jade pedestal. Opens to reveal inner egg of Imperial jade, which in turn opens to display 12 assorted diamonds, 4 yellows, 4 blues, and 4 whites, totaling 300 carats. Easter gift from Peter the Great to Catherine I. Value $3,500,000.

Of the four items only the Spanish Dagger could not have been concealed in a coffee or sugar can. Carlota's

Rosary and the item called Lady's Ring could easily have been hidden thus. Likewise Catherine's Egg.

In the actual event, Charles Louis Urquhart and his accomplice had found the Spanish Dagger and the Lady's Ring and were searching for something else, which would have to be Carlota's Rosary or Catherine's Egg. Or both, of course. The last time I had seen it, the Rosary was wrapped around Alice's elegant waist.

But where was Catherine's Egg? And why hadn't Alice told me about all this? She'd given me an explanation only for her possession of the Rosary, the Dagger, and the ruby ring: heirlooms. But no mention at all of Catherine's Egg, a mere $3,500,000 oversight. And when she'd said that her mother died about six months ago, leaving her these heirlooms, she had *not* said that her mother was raped, robbed, and murdered.

"Learn anything?" Sweeney asked. I must have gone into trance, thinking of a $500,000 rosary, a $50,000 dagger, a $10,000 ring, and a $3,500,000 egg, for I heard him as from a great distance. He asked again, "Did you learn anything?"

"Sorry," I said. "Yes, one thing I learned. There's no way those things from the Beverly Hills robbery could connect up to last night's attempted burglary."

A noble effort, but useless. Sweeney wasn't one to be led easily by the nose. It could be done, but not easily.

He said, "Nevertheless, they do connect up, Streeter. The man you killed was involved in the Beverly Hills robbery, maybe not as an accomplice, but he was there. So what was he looking for last night? That's the question. Would this Alice be the sort of young lady to know such persons?"

"Absolutely not," I said. "She lives like a nun."

"Well, we'll find out," he said, "when she comes back Thursday. You said she'll definitely be here for rehearsals?"

"Yes."

"Meanwhile, maybe we'll luck out. Maybe she'll hear the news, or read a paper. She'd call, wouldn't she?"

"Oh, certainly. Alice is the soul of conscientiousness. She'd get in touch at once."

Unless she's picked up first, I was thinking. Or unless the fat burglar or the mysterious third man got to her.

"Funny thing about that list," Sweeney said.

Unthinkingly I put my hand into my coat pocket, feeling for the Lady's Ring, but it wasn't there because I wasn't wearing the same jacket I'd had on when I slipped the ring off Urquhart's pinkie and dropped it in my pocket.

"So what's funny about the list?" I asked.

"The Spanish Dagger," said Sweeney. "The list describes it as a two-edged blade."

"What about it?"

"Well, you said the knife you killed the burglar with had a two-edged blade, right? The wound showed a two-edged . . ."

"Oh, it didn't look anything at all like the description on that list," I said.

"Still and all, most big knives are single-edged. You hardly ever see a two-edged blade. Very uncommon." He sighed deeply. "Well, it was just a thought."

And it would remain just a thought until he could interrogate Alice. I excused myself, saying I had to catch some sleep, and went up to Junep's apartment. I let myself in with the master keys. It had occurred to me that I'd better lock his bedroom window in case some snoop should happen to notice while prowling the fire escape. Then I went down to my apartment and got out the Manhattan yellow pages and looked under "Jewelers" for Count Carlo. He had a display ad, three double-column inches: *Jewelry by Carlo*—Paris, Rome, New York, Hollywood." The local address was in the Carnegie Hall block on 57th Street. The designer was famous, and anyone who riffled through the pages of the Sunday magazine section of the *New York Times* knew his name. He had designed jewelry for Hollywood stars and other royalty. He was seen regularly in the society pages. I recalled having seen his shop when I went for an occasional afternoon stroll. Today being Sunday, it would be closed. No matter, I had to have a look.

It was about nine o'clock when I hit the street. It was empty except for a pair of weary hookers sitting on the low wall of the little plaza across from McAnn's, which was closed till one P.M. on account of our sabbath blue laws.

Lieutenant Sweeney was just getting into his car when I came out of the building. I nodded to him and started to walk on by.

"Oh, Streeter!" he called. "Hold it!" I turned and walked over to the curb. He said, "Need a lift?"

"No thanks, Lieutenant," I said. "Just thought I'd take a little walk in the park, count the squirrels, try to forget last night . . ."

"Hop in. I'll drop you at the park entrance."

"Thanks anyway, Lieutenant. The walk'll be good for what ails me."

"And what's that, Streeter?"

Bulldog Sweeney, Terror of Evil-doers. He never let up. He had a way of making me feel as if he had me by the scruff of the neck. Actually, of course, it was the other way around. Bulldog Sweeney was slow. Let him clamp his jaws on a solid clue, however, and he'd tear a case apart.

"Like I told you," I said, "I need to forget last night. See you later. Take care, and get some rest."

He didn't insist, and I walked on. As I waited at the corner of Broadway for the light, I expected his car to catch up. It didn't. I glanced over my shoulder as I crossed the street and saw the car still parked in front of the club.

Times Square is a carnival queen at night, but on Sunday

mornings she looks and smells like an old whore with a wine hangover. Few street characters are out at nine A.M. on Sundays, but I saw Hellfire Henry getting an early start in front of Howard Johnson's. The tall, gaunt skypilot stood on his milk crate, a blazing-eyed Jeremiah haranguing a crowd of three persons on the subject of Heaven and Hell and the Sinful Snares of Satan. Usually his confederate, Badfoot George, would have been dipping the gentlemen's wallets and the ladies' handbags, but not in a crowd of three. Badfoot George was a little, old, white-haired black with a built-in smile like Louis Armstrong's, except that Badfoot couldn't turn his off. Along with the permanent smile he wore a Purple Heart, his consolation prize for the war-shattered foot. I waited on the corner until I caught his eye. I beckoned him over. He came limping and smiling.

"Mr. Joe Streeter!" he said. We slapped hands. "What you doin' up and about so early in the mornin'?"

"Looking for Alice."

"One of the girls?"

"She's the cigarette girl at my club. She also does the disappearing-girl bit in the magic show."

"Gotcha. Some of us was watchin' the show last night. Heard you gonna be on regular Saturday nights."

"That's right. Did you watch *The Cabinet of Doctor Caligari?*"

"The magic show? Sure."

"Well, the disappearing girl disappeared. I have to find her before the wrong guys do. She's up to her ears in trouble."

"Anything to do with that burglar you killed last night? It's on the radio this mornin'. They say on the news a pickup-and-hold is out on her. So what she do, Mr. Streeter?"

"I don't know that she did anything, George. But I'll pay a bundle for information on where she's gone."

"Well, I ain't heard nothin' so far, Mr. Streeter, but I'll move around, see what I can find out."

I slipped him a sawbuck and thanked him. He went back to Hellfire Henry. There were half a dozen in his audience by now, enough for Badfoot to work on. As I headed up 7th Avenue the city car in front of Pal Joey's was still there. If Sweeney intended to tail me he'd have to do it on foot, because 7th Avenue runs one-way downtown and I was walking uptown. Of course, he could detour around the block and be waiting for me on Central Park South by the entrance to the park. If he took the bait he wouldn't see what I was up to on 57th Street. Not that I expected to do much of anything, but . . . I didn't want Sweeney to see me peering in Count Carlo's shop window.

As I turned right onto 57th Street, just for luck I looked back down the avenue and then up to the park, but I saw no one I could be sure was a cop except a pair of harness bulls standing on a corner.

The shop I was looking for was where I'd expected to find it, a little to the left of the Russian Tea Room, which in turn is a little to the left of Carnegie Hall. The facade of the jeweler's shop was solid yellow brick with two narrow windows flanking a large bronze door set back about four feet from the sidewalk. On the door was a plaque of polished brass. It read simply: *Carlo*.

Two of Count Carlo's pieces were on display, one in each window, a bracelet and a brooch. The designs of both pieces were elaborate, flamboyant, very much in the style of the ruby ring in the pocket of my dress jacket at home. These pieces in Count Carlo's windows were no doubt paste, or they wouldn't have been left for any smash-and-grab artist to take. It happens even in this part of town, where you have almost as many plainclothes and private cops on the street as you do in the diamond block down on 47th Street. It happened to Tiffany's, it could happen to

68

Carlo's. Though the display pieces must have been paste, security was heavy: thick double windows, alarm tapes around the outer panes, television cameras covering the outside of the shop immediately in front of the windows, and the big bronze door. The treasure was inside somewhere, and the safe would no doubt require a master cracksman.

In each window, besides the jewelry, there was an exhibition-mounted 8 x 10 colorphoto portrait of Count Car o himself. Each portrait was a profile, a left and a right, and in each picture one of his hands was visible in a lower corner, just enough to show his work, a finger ring in one photo, a bracelet in the other, elegantly baroque but presumably designed to be worn by men.

For once I was not interested in jewels. It was Count Carlo who interested me. There was no doubt in my mind as I studied the photo portraits; Count Carlo was the fat burglar who got away.

7

I should have looked him up in the white pages while I was looking for him in the commercial directory, but my Model T brain was only sparking three cylinders this morning. So I walked east to the Horn & Hardart near the corner of the Avenue of the Americas. The automat had a bank of telephones and directories for all five boroughs. I checked the Manhattan book first and found a couple dozen Carlos, which I dialed in alphabetical order, but of those who answered none were counts. I thought about the other four directories. There had to be a better way. Bubba Antrim.

I had told him last night he could phone me in the late morning and I'd fill him in on *l'affaire* Pal Joey's. It was not yet nine-thirty, but I tried. A recording asked me to leave my name and number. I said it was Joe Streeter and I'd call him later. On second thought I said he shouldn't call me. I couldn't be sure who was answering the phones at the club and my apartment.

I bought the Sunday papers at the corner stand and headed for Central Park, dumping everything but the en-

tertainment sections in the first trash basket I came to. I
found a sunny bench along the path that runs behind the
park wall and got into the reviews. Bubba Antrim's was the
rave he'd promised. He especially admired Alice's "incredi-
bly accurate impersonations" and called her "a woman for
all seasons." The other reviewers were equally enthusiastic.
I tore out the reviews, folded them, and slipped them in my
coat pocket for Alice to read when I caught up with her. I
sat there for a while, basking in the morning sunshine and
the fine reviews. A dog-walker went by with a brace of
graceful salukis, an English bulldog that looked like
Sweeney, and a pair of big Bouviers on a handful of leashes.
The dog-walker looked rather like Alice, shoulder-length
dark brown hair, Spanish eyes, and a nice figure, not Alice's
mind-boggling build but a real eyeballer nonetheless. I
wanted very badly to find Alice. I watched a squirrel turning
somersaults on the grass only a few yards from the dog-
walker and her dogs. She managed all five with soft words
and gentle tugs on their leashes. The salukis and the Bouviers were straining after the squirrel, who flicked his tail and
somersaulted happily, probably baiting the dogs. The two
pairs would have carried the girl away, but she spoke to the
English bulldog and kicked him gently in the rump and he
pulled on his leash in the direction away from the salukis
and the Bouviers. Some handling, I thought, and I wondered about Alice. Was she handling? I couldn't see her
acting at random. Crazy she might be, but not stupid.

The squirrel suddenly stopped its acrobatics and ran up
an oak tree. The dog-walker and her dogs went on down
the path toward the Sheep Meadow. Watching them go, I
remembered Schatzi, my silvery German shepherd, and
how we used to romp in the park. She'd been shot and
killed by the same hitter who aced my partner the year
before. I'd been wanting to get another shepherd like
Schatzi ever since, and whenever I went to the park and

watched the dogs I promised myself I'd do it. Now I swore I'd do it before the week was out.

Though it was only nine blocks down to my street, I took a taxi. Heart of a lion, and all that, but I was tired. The cabbie was a spieler and started in at once chattering about the Fourth of July fireworks display to be staged on the Hudson opposite the 79th Street marina, and he was getting into the tragedy of a few years earlier when the fireworks barge blew up and killed several men. What is it with cab drivers and barbers, they have to talk? I told him to let me down at the Hotel Taft.

A couple of friends of mine were standing on the corner, Nickels Detroit and Mister Magoo, both of them ex-hoofers from the Cotton Club years. I never knew Detroit's right name, unless that was it. Nickels was a nickname, of course, acquired when inflation forced him to peddle five-dollar bags of reefer instead of his previous dimes. Of late the gentry around Times Square had taken to calling him Joints Detroit, or simply The Joint, because inflation had struck again, forcing him to abandon the nickel bag and begin peddling loose joints at a dollar each, six for five.

Mister Magoo's right name was Sylvester Beamish. He'd been known as Specks until he threw away his glasses because glaucoma had made him stone blind. His buddy Detroit couldn't walk very well because he'd suffered a bad stroke that left his legs swollen like enormous sausages. But Magoo was still strong, so Detroit would lean on him and direct him through traffic. Mister Magoo carried the stash, Detroit handled the cash.

They were in the process of turning some loose joints when I came along. I waited by the curb until the deal had gone down, then walked up to them.

"Loose joints," Detroit said. "Dollar apiece, pure Colombian gold. Six for five, and a good count. Three for two to you, Mr. Streeter." I gave him a double sawbuck. He told Magoo, "Thirty joints to Mr. Streeter, and don't fumble."

"I'll fumble *you,* motherfucker," Mister Magoo said.

That was the thing about his bad mouth, never cursed or said a dirty word but motherfucker, which he used indiscriminately and at all times, except to ladies. It was said that he used it on a lady once, Broadway Rose, if in fact she was a lady and not a transvestite as was generally believed. Either way Mister Magoo was right about her. She was one bad mother. Her shtick was to hook a john and lure him into an alleyway for a quickie standing up, or to a rooftop for something more leisurely, and there she'd get his pants down, whip out a straight razor, and threaten to cut his dick off if he resisted. She'd relieve him of his wallet or anything else of value, then cut off his dick anyway or back him over the edge of the roof. When Mister Magoo was younger, when he was still known as Specks, before he danced off the apron of the Apollo stage and fell into a kettledrum, he called Broadway Rose a motherfucker one night in the old Jack Dempsey's, and she told him if he didn't apologize she'd carve him like a Christmas turkey right there in the restaurant. Such was her reputation, he apologized, and he never insulted a lady after that. Sometime later Broadway Rose fell off a roof herself, or so they say, but then you hear a lot of stories around Times Square. Some say she's still working.

Mister Magoo said, "I hope you appreciate good smoke, motherfucker."

"I'm sure the smoke is fine," I said. "But I'm looking for something else. Keep the joints."

"We heard," Detroit said. "Badfoot told us. You think something happened to the girl? Maybe she's hiding out?"

"I don't know," I said. "But I've got to find her. There may be some heavies looking for her. If you hear . . ."

"We'll ask around," Detroit said.

Magoo said, "That a fact you killed a burglar in the club last night, motherfucker?" He was giving me the blind look that got him his nickname, standing close to me and peering up out of empty eyes. "It got anything to do with Alice?"

"Well, the burglar was in her apartment," I said. "There was a second burglar, but he got away. She may be hiding from him, but I doubt it. She could have stayed where she was. He couldn't get to her. His name is Count Carlo, and he has a jewelry shop on 57th Street a little east of the Russian Tea Room. The cops don't know this. I want to talk to him before they do."

"What's happening, motherfucker?"

"Get me some information on Alice's whereabouts, and I'll tell you the whole story," I said.

Mister Magoo laughed and said, "Gimme some skin, motherfucker."

He held out his hand, palm up, and I slapped it. Then I laid a double sawbuck in it.

"What is it, a deuce, motherfucker?"

"It's a twenty," Detroit said. "That makes two."

We all slapped hands around and I walked on. I could see from the corner of 7th Avenue and 50th Street that Lieutenant Sweeney's city car was still in front of the club. He'd been getting ready to drive off, I thought, when I was leaving. I wondered if he was as tired as I. As I walked up the street a big liner hooted its enormous horn, like the thunderous roar of a friendly Tyrannosaurus Rex. I could see the great ship moving grandly upstream, passing the river end of the street, hooting hello to New York.

Sweeney wasn't in the club when I got there. A few other detectives were hanging around. Judging from the smell, they'd been into my bar. They were all smoking cigars or cigarettes, but you could still smell the bourbon. The usual corps of cleaning ladies were at their morning's work with brooms, mops, and polishing cloths. I went to the bar and got out the cognac and a glass. One of the ladies was polishing the back end of the bar.

"Excuse me, sir," she said. "I'll just start in at the front end."

She took her cloths and lemon oil and went to the other end and began polishing. I hadn't noticed Stacy and Colleen sitting in the back corner at my private table. They got up and went to the stage and started a song-and-dance routine. I watched it while I sipped the brandy. It was a new bit, or a variation on their old routine, Stacy singing blues *a capella* and Colleen shuffling soft-shoe with an occasional tap for emphasis.

The cuckoo clock over the backbar sang out: ten thirty. The cleaning lady polishing the bar had nearly worked her way to where I was. The smell of lemon oil was strong. I would have preferred Alice's scent, or Harriet Maxwell's perfume, Tigresse. Or anything but lemon oil.

I couldn't drink with that smell in the room, and anyway it was time to try Bubba Antrim again, so I got off my bar stool to go to the phone.

The cleaning lady said, "Don't bother to move, sir."

She smiled a grandmotherly smile and brushed a wisp of gray hair from her forehead. I didn't recognize her until she spoke, and then, to corn a phrase, I nearly jumped out of my skin.

8

I knocked back the rest of my drink and said, loudly, for the detectives to hear, "Come with me, ma'am. I want you to do the greenroom today."

"Yes, sir," Alice said. Her voice cracked and quavered. She sounded ninety years old. "I'll be right with you, sir." She moved slowly, gathering her polishing cloths. "Right with you, Mr. Streeter." Groaning a little, she hobbled to the front end of the bar and got her purse, a very large old-fashioned reticule. She came back and picked up the mop and pail. "It's a pleasure," she said, "to meet you vis-à-vis, Mr. Streeter, after working here all these years, a real pleasure, sir. When I was younger I was in show business myself. I danced in the line at the Roxy, and once in a real Broadway show . . ."

"Come along," I told her.

"Yes, sir."

She carried the pail and mop and the big reticule as if the load were killing her, and the detectives were eyeing me as if I were some kind of uncouth beast, letting a poor little old lady carry all that by herself. I ignored them and led the way downstairs. The greenroom was empty. I locked the door, then checked Matt Griffin's bedroom, the old office. He was out, probably visiting his lady friend. Seventy-odd and he had a sweetheart in her sixties whom he visited afternoons and nights off. Alice began to remove her disguise, taking off the old lady's bonnet, unbuttoning the high-necked blouse, kicking off the clumpy work shoes. She wasn't looking at me as she disrobed. I waited for her to speak, since she had a lot to say, but she wasn't saying anything. So I got to the point.

"Why did you disappear again? Don't lie!"

"I went to mass."

I slapped her face and felt like a sadist slapping a little old lady.

"I said don't lie!"

"But it's true, Joey. I did go to mass."

"Where?"

"Why?"

"Never mind why! Tell me where?"

"Saint Paul's, over by Sixtieth Street and . . ."

"Damn it! I *know* where it is! Why there?"

"But I go everywhere, Joey. Last Sunday, let's see, I went to the Church of the Blessed Sacrament up on Seventy-first Street. Do you know where that one is, darling? East of Sherman Square? It's a very beautiful church, in the gothic style, with a rose window . . ."

"What was your mother's name?"

"Are you interrogating me, Officer?"

"Your damned right, I am!"

"Please don't shout, Joey." Outraged innocence. It looked real, really real. I stuffed my hands into my pants pockets for fear I'd slap her again. She looked up at me with that look of outraged innocence, and I didn't believe it. I wanted to take her in my arms and kiss her, and like that.

77

"Joey," she said, "please don't jingle the coins in your pocket that way." I realized that's what I'd been doing, nervously jingling the coins in my right trouser pocket. "It reminds me of something frightening that happened to me when I was a little girl in Veracruz," she said. "And ever since then, it makes me nervous to see a man jingling the coins in his pants pocket."

"All right," I said. "Tell me about it."

"A small circus came to town," she said, "and there was a clown. Well, I was wandering around the animal cages and I saw a man talking to the tiger. He told me to come closer and he'd introduce me to the tiger, so I did, because I wanted to know the tiger. I noticed he was jingling coins in his big, baggy pants, and I thought he was just being a clown, you know, so when he told me to put my hand in his pocket and I'd find a surprise, I did. And ever since then it makes me nervous . . ."

"What was your mother's name?"

"Mamá was the Principessa Francesca di Casoli. Why are you asking, Joey?"

"That's Italian. Your name is Spanish."

"Please, Joey, this isn't the Inquisition, you know. Mamá was born María Juana Francisca Gómez Sandoval, in Tlaquepaque, a *colonia* of Guadalajara. She was a *tapatía*, you know, born in the state of Jalisco. My father was José Luis Farah Peñaloza, a horse breeder from Durango. They went to live in Veracruz, and I was born there. When Papá died I was only a few months old. When I was two, Mamá married the Italian consul, Príncipe Gianni di Casoli, and when I was three he died. I don't remember the prince very clearly, only that I loved him. Why are you asking me all these questions, Joey?"

"What about Catherine's Egg?"

"Oh, that!" she said. "Now I understand. Well, I've managed to recover part of Mamá's jewels—Carlota's Rosary . . . It's just that I didn't want to talk about it, Joey, because I still haven't gotten over the shock. Mamá didn't die a natural death, you see . . . Oh, it's too horrible! Please, Joey, do I have to?"

"We'll go upstairs," I said. "Put your clothes on. You're going as the little old cleaning lady again."

"You're so understanding, Joey," she said.

She smiled brightly and threw her arms around me and kissed me. She still had on the gray wig and the Old Lady makeup. Some sexy Old Lady. And so there seemed to be no great hurry about going up to my apartment, for after all, we were alone here in the greenroom. The door was locked. We had all the comforts of home, including a wide black leather couch. She looked very strange when she was out of her costume, the 19-year-old's body and the Old Lady's gray hair and wrinkled face. I felt rather odd. I told myself that behind the wrinkles there was Alice. There was also Garbo, Dietrich, Monroe, and Helen of Troy. And I began to believe it. Soon I could see it, I could see behind the mask. But what I saw behind the mask of makeup was another mask, and that one was the Alice of Pal Joey's, the cigarette girl. Persona behind persona. I didn't know her at all. We were on the couch when I'd got this far, and that's as far as I got.

"It's no good," I told her. "You'll have to take off the makeup. Not now. We'll go upstairs. Get back into the Old Lady costume."

Obviously I was having a 49-year-old problem with a 19-year-old. I knew it, and I hated it.

We went up the inside stairway, bypassing the club. There were no detectives now on the stairs or the landings. Had Junep's body been discovered, there would have been legions of cops.

When we got to my apartment Alice went straight to the bedroom, pulled off the bonnet and the gray wig and

79

stripped to the buff. Then she sat at the dressing table and began to remove the makeup. She still wore Carlota's Rosary around her lovely, kissable waist.

I thought to escape from my personal problem by getting at Alice's.

"You were saying you recovered part of your mother's jewels," I began. "Tell me more about that. How did you do it?"

"Please, Joey," she said, looking at me in the mirror with those soulful Spanish eyes surrounded by gobs of cold cream and smeared gray wrinkles. "Do I have to talk about it? You have no idea how distressing . . ."

"Alice, you're going to have to tell me *all* about it," I said. "I've been protecting you so far, but if I'm going to handle this, I need to know more. I need to know what we're up against, *whom* we're up against. Tell me about the night of the robbery in Beverly Hills."

"Oh, Joey," she said. "That's the worst part! I don't know if I *can* talk about it."

"If you *can?*" I said. "You can *act* your way through it!" I believed it. I thought she could act her way through anything, probably her own hanging. She was the consummate actress, always onstage. She probably staged her own dreams when she slept. She once told me that she hadn't learned everything she knew in the UCLA dramatic arts courses. Since she was a little girl playing with dolls in Veracruz, she'd been designing costume and doing makeup, creating characters and even roles. She was a natural. I said, "Alice, two men tried to kill me last night, maybe three men, so you're going to answer my questions, sweetheart, or I'm going to put you over my knee and spank your pretty bottom until it's red, white, and blue."

She was working cold cream into the Old Lady makeup, nearly ready to wipe it off. She looked at me in the mirror, and she saw I meant business. But still she had to try.

"Oh, Joey, please! Do I have to?"

Even under the mess of smeared makeup she managed to look appealing, sad, like a little lost girl. Really touching. I weakened.

"No," I said. "You don't have to. I already know what happened that night. But you can tell me how you recovered Carlota's Rosary. And how come you didn't get Catherine's Egg while you were about it?"

"All right," she said. "I'll tell you. Just a sec." She wiped away the cold cream with some tissues, then finished with a face towel. "You see, I never believed Mamá's escort that night was innocent," she said. "So when they let him go, I was waiting for him outside the Los Angeles County Courthouse, and I followed him. And I was right, he had the jewels. He tried to talk me into accepting part of the loot. Imagine! I pretended to go along, and that's how I got away with Carlota's Rosary, but I couldn't get Catherine's Egg. He only let me handle the Rosary."

"And the Spanish Dagger?"

"Well, yes, that too."

"And the ruby ring?"

"Yes."

"Well, damn it, why didn't you say so?"

"I was going to, Joey. I mean, all this is so upsetting, bringing it all back, how Mamá died . . ." She broke up, sitting naked and huddled on the dressing table bench, her face in her hands, crying her big beautiful brown eyes out. "You're just being cruel," she murmured. "Why are you doing this to me, Joey?"

"Who has Catherine's Egg now?"

"What do you mean?"

"You want that spanking?"

"Joey, how could I know where the Egg is? Charles had it. He must have hidden it somewhere."

"He burgled your apartment looking for it. He didn't find it."

"What are you saying, Joey?"

"Don't act dumb! He thought you had it. He must have had reason to think so."

"Reason? Joey, are you calling Charles Louis Urquhart a reasonable man? He was insane, an insane killer. He wasn't looking for the Egg. He was looking for *me!* To kill me the way he murdered Mamá!" She slid off the dressing table bench, moaning and sobbing, and lay huddled on the floor. I waited. Presently she looked up at me with tragic eyes. "Do you know what that man did to her?"

"Urquhart offed it on somebody else," I said, "a black man . . ."

"No, Joey! He did it alone! Don't you see? No witnesses . . ."

"Well," I said, "what's done is done. If he stole the Egg, he hid it somewhere. We'll have to do what we can with what we have."

I felt pretty silly saying all those clichés. What's done is never done, in fact, and as for doing what we can with what we have, what in hell else does anyone do all the time? But the hurt in Alice's eyes gave place to hope, and she flung her arms around my legs and held me tight.

"We?" she asked. "You said we?" I knelt by her and took her face between my hands and kissed her. "Oh, Joey!" she said softly, all dewy-eyed. "We!"

"Urquhart had a partner," I said. "He was a short, fat Italian. Know him?"

"No, I don't think so, love. What about him?"

"We exchanged a few shots last night, but he got away. I've been doing some sleuthing, and I know who he is."

I stood up, pulling her up with me. We got comfortable, with our arms around each other. I was still fully dressed, while Alice wore only the Rosary. She seemed to spend a

82

lot of time in the buff. Nakedest woman I'd ever known, with one exception, a shake dancer in the Club Cachassa, which is a big joint on the Belem waterfront, at the mouth of the Amazon. She called herself La Bomba, and she danced with nothing on but a conga drum slung around her neck by a thong. Alice brought my wandering mind back to the moment with one slim leg deftly slid between mine.

She said, "So who is he, Joey?"

"Count Carlo, jewel designer to high society, with shops in Paris, Rome, New York, and Hollywood."

"Why, Mamá knew him!" Alice cried. "For heaven's sake, Count Carlo designed her ruby ring!"

"But you never knew him?"

"Well, I may have met him at one of Mamá's parties. One couldn't possibly remember every person one met, you know, Mamá was such a socialite. I really couldn't stand it. I hardly ever stayed at home, though I loved Mamá. But you see, she was no longer young, and she felt she had to take her pleasure where she could find it, which explains Charles . . ."

"Well," I said, "this Count Carlo seemed to know *you.*"

"Oh?"

"Yes. I overheard him and Charles talking before I let myself into your apartment. Charles said something to the effect that 'it' wasn't there, 'just this goddamn knife and the ring,' and then he said he didn't think you'd keep it there anyway because you're not stupid. And then Count Carlo said, 'No, Charles, she's not stupid, she's crazy.' So how come Count Carlo knows you so well."

Before I could prevent her, she had flung away from me, reached into the cold cream jar, and slapped me with a handful of the grease. Too late, I grabbed her wrists. She howled like a banshee and tried to bite me. I took her wrists in my left hand and slapped her with my right. That stopped her biting me. She snarled like a tigress.

83

"Crazy, am I? You beast, I'll give you crazy! You fiend! You Simon Legree! You Hitler!"

I held her wrists behind her back with one hand while I snatched up a face towel and wiped the grease off my head, with her shrieking and cursing at me all the while, and when I had most of the mess wiped away I laid her on the shag carpet. She struggled at first, but I had both her wrists in one hand, leaving my other free. Presently she relaxed, then began to help, and after that we set an all-time record, after which we lay gasping like beached salmon in spawning season. I could have fallen asleep then and there, and indeed was already nodding off, but Alice moved under me, and then there was no question of sleep. Sometime later we went into the bathroom, where I finished taking off my clothes.

When we were in the shower I said, "It looks to me like Count Carlo's our man. Urquhart wasn't very bright, didn't even have a gun, came at me with that big knife. He knew how to hold it flat so it would go between the ribs, but he must have figured that being so big himself and knowing how to hold a blade he was invincible. It takes more. You must have the will. I don't think Charles was a killer." Alice was saying nothing, just listening and soaping. We were soaping each other. "I have a hunch," I said. "I think Count Carlo has Catherine's Egg."

"Hm?" she said, and went on with her soaping.

"I think he found it," I said, "either in the coffee can or the sugar or flour container in your kitchen." She stopped soaping me. I went right on doing her. "I think you lied to me, baby doll."

"Oh, Joey," she said, sitting down on the tiles while the shower played over her, "what can I say, love? I didn't want to get you involved in all this." She raised up onto her knees and put her arms around my thighs. "Those are dangerous men, Joey, and I didn't want you to get hurt. I

84

didn't tell you about the Egg because I wanted to protect you, and I knew you'd get involved if you knew about it. You'd try to help me, and you might get hurt. I love you, Joey."

"So tell me the truth if you love me."

"I will. I'll tell you the truth. I did get the Egg and the Dagger and the ruby ring back from Charles. Not just Carlota's Rosary but everything he'd stolen from Mamá. That's why he came after me last night."

She was wearing the Rosary, and the shower streamed down her body and over the pearls and amethysts and the silver Christ hanging in her soapy black bush.

"Don't you ever take that thing off?" I asked her.

"Does it make you nervous, Joey?"

"Yes."

"Oh? I hadn't noticed."

"Touché. Who do you think pulled the Dagger out of Charles?"

She stood up, and we began rinsing the soap off one another.

"Count Carlo?"

"Possibly," I said. "He could have come back after I chased him up to the roof. I went back to your apartment then, and the Dagger was still sticking in Charles. When I returned a short time later with Lieutenant Sweeney, the Dagger was gone. Now, here's an odd thing. Charles Louis Urquhart and Count Carlo weren't alone. Someone, not Carlo, shot Charles in the back while I was fighting him for the Dagger. The shot had to come from your bedroom or from the bedroom window. So there was a third person, and he could have come back later and taken the Dagger."

"Yes, I see," she said. We were carefully rinsing the soap out of each other's nooks and crannies, and we were beginning to breathe heavily again. She said, "Have you any idea who he could be, this third man?"

"Terence D. Moran."

"Who?"

"Charles was carrying a driver's license in the name of Terence D. Moran."

"You've got me confused, Joey. Do we have to go into all this right now? I've got a better idea . . ." She had certainly got hold of something. I took her hands in mine. She looked up at me. "All right," she said. "Who is this Terence D. Moran, and why was Charles carrying Moran's driver's license?"

"That's my question," I said. "Anyway, if Moran was the one who shot Charles in the back and later took the Spanish Dagger out of him, he's probably the one who hit Herb Junep on the head and then stabbed him with a large two-edged blade."

"Herbie?" she said softly. She began to tremble. She laid her head against my chest, and I released her hands and held her close. Her whole body was trembling. "Not Herbie! What happened, Joey? My God, don't tell me Herbie's dead!"

"And the blade is missing again."

"Joey! I'm scared!"

She was weeping, and I held her while she wept. Did she weep, though? We were still standing under the shower, and she was sobbing. But did she weep? And if she wept, was it for Herb Junep?

I said, "My apartment was broken into."

"My God, what's happening, Joey? Was anything stolen?"

"I don't think so. I haven't made a careful search, but I think I must have scared the burglar away before he had time to steal anything. Anyway, I haven't got anything of value that a burglar would be likely to try and steal. A couple of antique musical instruments, not highly portable, Saturday's receipts in the safe, but that safe's an antique too, solid iron and hard to crack. I think the burglar was someone who knows about you and me, somebody who doesn't know that Count Carlo found the Egg when he burgled your apartment. Whoever he is, he must have thought you stashed the Egg in my place."

Alice said, "Could he be this Terence Moran you mentioned?"

"Maybe. But why would he kill Junep? Assuming that the same person who took the Dagger out of Charles also stuck it in Junep . . . No, I'm too tired," I said. "It'll have to wait."

"You seem pretty lively to me," Alice said.

"Too tired for thinking," I said. "Not too tired altogether."

"So let's go to bed."

I turned off the shower.

9

A cluster of aerial bombs burst over Times Square, waking us at noon. We'd had little sleep, but we woke refreshed. After a brief dalliance we got up, showered again, no nonsense this time, and prepared breakfast together, eggs and sausages, pancakes and plenty of butter and maple syrup, lots of coffee. I tried to question Alice again, but she put up some heavy resistance. Not now, she said. She couldn't eat a bite of breakfast if she had to talk about all that. I let up on her.

After breakfast I phoned Lieutenant Sweeney, tracking him through the Midtown Precinct North switchboard. I asked him when his people would be finished working in and around the club, and he said not until tomorrow sometime. A special team from the LAPD were arriving tonight to make their own investigation, since the NYPD ballistics report had tied the bullet in Charles Louis Urquhart's back to the cop killing in Los Angeles six months ago. I thanked him and started to hang up.

"While I've got you, Streeter," he said, "let me ask, have

you heard from the young lady, María de los Ángeles something or other? God! the names they pick."

"Not a word," I said. "I assume she's still in Atlantic City."

"And she doesn't read the papers?"

"Why should she? She's taking a vacation."

"But today's papers are reporting on your club's television show last night. They all speak highly of her part in the magic show. And since when doesn't an actress read her own reviews? And if she reads the reviews, she has to see the story on page one of all the papers: 'Joe Streeter, jazz pianist and owner of Pal Joey's, killed a burglar last night in the apartment of María what's-her-name, known as Alice, a performer in the club, et cetera.' So what about it, Streeter?"

"You don't know Alice. She couldn't care less. Remember, she didn't come back onstage for her bows either."

"Huh!" He grunted and grumbled, then said, "Yeah, okay, you're right, I see your point. Well, I guess it takes all kinds in show business."

I said, "That *is* show biz."

"Well, I shouldn't be surprised," he said. "I've met nothing but oddballs since I've been working the theater district."

I don't think the actor lives, has lived or will ever live, who willingly would forgo his bow or cares nothing for reviews. Actors live for recognition. As for Lieutenant Sweeney's gratuitous rudeness, I hung up on him.

Having overheard the conversation, or my end of it, Alice asked when the cops would be gone from the premises. I told her the LAPD was sending a special team to make an independent investigation of last night's affair. There'd be cops on the scene until sometime tomorrow, if not longer.

"Sweeney asked if I'd heard from you," I said. "You heard what I told him."

"Thanks, Joey. What was that about my not taking a bow?"

"He knows about the switch ending to your act."

"What switch ending?"

"When you didn't reappear after Caligari opened and closed the cabinet half a dozen times, he wanted to go down to the greenroom and see what had happened to you. We both thought you'd been hurt somehow by the trapdoor or the lift. Anyway, Caligari had a brainstorm. He went into the cabinet himself and shut the door. I told Dom to have the stagehands dismantle and remove the cabinet immediately. The audience liked it. I think we'll keep it in."

"So John didn't come back for the bow either?"

"That was the switch: girl and magician *both* disappear. Completely. A new twist on an old turn."

"I see."

"Anyway, Sweeney was a little suspicious. He would be, of course. Suspicion is a way of life with detectives. Nothing is simply what it seems. It has to be something else."

"He's right," Alice said.

"Anyway, he's got a pickup-and-hold on you."

"What did *I* do, for God's sake? I didn't kill anybody."

"It's only for questioning in connection with the burglary. The lieutenant wants to know what the burglars were after, and whether they got it. He suspects a jewel scam because Urquhart's prints tie him into the Beverly Hills robbery-homicide, and he doesn't believe in mere coincidence."

"That's why they're sending a special team of investigators from Los Angeles?"

"That," I said, "and the bullet in Urquhart's back. It came from a gun used in a Los Angeles bank robbery in which a cop was killed. The robber took the cop's gun. If he was here last night and shot Urquhart, then maybe he

90

was involved also in the Beverly Hills jewel heist. He could be the man who robbed, raped, and murdered your mother."

If my blunt approach to the matter seemed cruel, it was so in a way that eluded me at the moment. I thought I knew what I was doing. Alice had not been very forthcoming in her explanations. My blunt statement seemed to strike her with physical force. She stood staring dumbly at me while her eyes filled with tears. Her lower lip trembled.

In a small voice she said, "Lieutenant Sweeney wants to question *me* about all that?"

"Yes."

"My God! Why?"

"Look at it this way," I said. "The police may be able to help you get back the stolen pieces, Catherine's Egg and the Spanish Dagger."

"No!" she said. "I can't risk it, Joey. The original owners, the Hapsburgs, maybe the Mexican government . . . It's been three generations, but still they may have a claim. I don't know about these things, Joey. I've got to get those jewels back without the police."

"Then you'll have to stay out of sight," I told her.

"You mean stay *here*? Just wait and do *nothing*?"

"I'll take care of it," I said. "I think I can get Catherine's Egg back for you, and maybe the Spanish Dagger."

"What about the ruby ring?"

That struck me as funny. She's wearing a $500,000 string of pearls and amethysts around her waist, and I'm offering to retrieve a $3,500,000 Russian Easter Egg, not to mention a $50,000 dagger, and she's counting small change, a mere $10,000 finger ring. There must be a word for that.

"All right," I said. "I don't think the Hapsburgs or the Mexican government will miss these baubles. Max and Carlota certainly won't. I don't know the law in these matters either, but if the jewels have been in your family for three generations, maybe your claim has some legitimacy. Who knows? Who cares? The reality, sweetheart, is that *you* have possession of Carlota's Rosary. Depending on how we handle it, you can realize quite a lot of money from the sale. If I can get you the right buyer, so we don't have to break up the rosary, you might realize full value, the entire half million." I went to the clothes closet and took the ruby ring out of the dress jacket I'd worn the night before. When she saw it, her eyes lit up like a child's on Christmas morning. She held out her hand. I slipped it on her third finger. "Here's an earnest," I said. "I'll get the other things for you."

She turned the ring about, letting the rubies catch the light.

"How did you get it, Joey?"

"I took it off Urquhart's little finger."

"Why didn't you take the Dagger too?"

"I couldn't think of a way to explain it to the police. But I did consider taking it. I didn't know how you were involved in all this, and I wanted to protect your interest, whatever it was. I also took what I thought was Urquhart's wallet. It turned out to be Terence D. Moran's, with his California driver's license in it. Urquhart wasn't carrying any ID of his own." Alice was still admiring the ring, turning it this way and that, enjoying the rubies' deep glow. I said, "This Terence D. Moran could be some shnook who lost his wallet, or he could be the man who shot Urquhart in the back. He could also be the bank robber and cop killer the LAPD are looking for. Funny thing about Moran's license, the physical description tallies almost perfectly with Charles Louis Urquhart's: age, height, weight, hair color. Only the eye color is different. So Urquhart *could* have been using Moran's license for ID. It would probably pass."

Alice went to the window and turned the rubies in the bright sunlight. I said, "If you disappear again, sweetheart, it might be for keeps this time. You're going to have to stay here in the apartment until this blows over."

"But I've got to *do* something!" she said, turning away from the window and facing me. "I can't just sit here waiting for one of those men to find me and kill me!" She rushed into my arms. "Oh, Joey, you've got me so frightened! Who *is* Moran? What does he want with *me?* I never even heard his name before. Joey, you've got to help me. *Do* something about those men!"

"I'll do what needs doing," I told her. "You stay here, lie low, don't answer the telephone or the doorbell."

"Joey, you're not going to leave me?"

"You'll be safe here," I told her. "The hall doors are triple-locked with chain lock, deadbolt, and police lock. So is the back door. And I nailed the porch windows shut."

"Where are you going?"

"To see about retrieving the Egg and the Dagger, and then try to peddle them and the Rosary. You should keep the ring. It's *you.*"

"You're sweet," she said. "But Joey, never mind the Egg and the Dagger, just see what you can get for the Rosary."

"I don't understand," I said. "The Egg's the prize."

"I'm afraid, Joey. I have to get some money, get away, go someplace—until it's over . . ."

She was breaking down again. Her voice shook with near-hysteria. Her whole body trembled. I felt her heartbeat quicken.

"It'll be all right," I said.

I was whistling in the dark. I had a little anxiety myself, what with a rape-strangler and cop-killer on the loose. The maniac probably knew where to find me at all times. He could walk in shadows, while I had to move in light. If he considered me a possible danger to him . . . Why, then, I had better move fast.

I told Alice to take a pill and get some sleep, but as I left her I wondered if she'd still be there when I got back. Assuming of course that I was coming back.

10

From a street phone I called Heinz Morgenlicht at his apartment in Essex House and told him I absolutely had to have an immediate viewing of last night's videotapes.

"It's Sunday," he said. "Why does it have to be today, Mr. Streeter?"

"It has something to do with what happened last night," I told him. "I'd rather not explain on the phone."

"So this is for the police?"

"I won't know till I view the tapes."

"Very well. I will arrange it for you. It's one o'clock now. Meet me in one hour at my office."

I thanked him, hung up, and dialed Bubba Antrim's private line at the Algonquin. This time he answered. I told him I had to see him right away. He said to come up and join him for brunch. It was only a few short blocks, and the day was fine, so I walked through Times Square eyeballing the country girls in town for the movie matinees. The marquees offered several kinds of trash, and of course the queues ran half around the block. Hellfire Henry and Badfoot George had moved their scene to the little island in Times Square called Father Duffy Square, and there under the good padre's inscrutable smile they plied their trade, saving souls and relieving them of their wallets. I spoke to George. He'd heard nothing about Alice, he said, except that everybody he asked seemed to know who she was, Joe Streeter's girl of the moment and an actress at Pal Joey's. I decided not to tell him she'd come back. He didn't need to know.

I passed Nathan's and felt like a survivor, remembering Toffenetti's and that grand strawberry shortcake. *Où sont les neiges d'antan,* right? Times Square itself will not long be with us. The city dads are going to tear down the whole damn neighborhood and erect monuments to hypocrisy in their own mindless image. I was feeling low enough to walk under a snake without stooping.

Lawrence Barbour Antrim had lived in the same suite at the old Hotel Algonquin for thirty years. It was said that he paid no rent because he attracted so much celebrity business. Everybody wanted to get close to New York's leading high-life columnist. He knew everybody, dead or alive. More important for my purposes, he knew where all the bones were buried.

"I was about to call you," he said as he let me in. "You beat me to the phone. Have you had breakfast? Brunch, perhaps?"

"I ate a little while ago," I said. "But I'll have coffee with you. And a cognac, if you don't mind."

He phoned his breakfast order to the dining room. We went into his parlor, a high-ceilinged room about twenty by thirty feet. It hadn't changed during his thirty years' occupancy. Indeed, it hadn't changed since the hotel was built seventy-five years before. The suite still had its original woodwork, the same old large-size fixtures, the fine parquet. The furniture was also fin de siècle, all hand-carved

96

mahogany. Only the bar and the piano were new. He had a semicircular wet bar and a Steinway grand. Bubba could play, with both hands, two fingers and eight thumbs. No matter, he loved doing it.

"I can scare up some coffee and cognac for you right here," he said as he went behind the bar. "Would you do me a favor, Joey? Tell me if my piano needs tuning? I don't hear as well as I did at your age, and I'm having some relatives from out of town tomorrow night, and one of them, my favorite cousin, is known back home in Schenectady for his Chopin. Frankly, I doubt that he plays any better than I do, but I pretend for his sake."

He was putting a pot of coffee together. I went to the piano and tried some chords and runs. Some of the fifths came out about four and a half. It was not only out of tune, the action was much too loose, and the tone was far too soft. It needed voicing, mechanical work, and tuning. Unlike Bubba's cousin I'm not known for my Chopin, but I can hear an ill-tempered pianoforte when I play one. How anyone could let a Steinway deteriorate so far outraged me. I wanted to lecture him on the care of mechanical instruments. However, I restrained my better nature. Bubba Antrim wasn't known for his sensitivity but for his fund of information on celebrities and for his connections.

I said, "For Chopin it could use a little work."

"Would you give me the name of your piano tuner?" he asked. "Mine has an ear infection and can't come today."

"I tune my own," I told him. "Use the yellow pages."

His piano tuner must have had the longest ear infection in the history of otolaryngology.

"Oh, you do?" Bubba said. "I hate to impose, and I know it's short notice, but would you mind, Joey?"

"Would I what?"

"Would you tune my Steinway for me? For *me?*"

He was being coquettish. Bubba Antrim was a country

gay, and like any smart country boy he could turn on the charm. He was a short man, about five feet seven, with close-cropped hair the color of dried blood, a bristly, bushy moustache of the same color, heavily wrinkled skin of a ruddy complexion, ears that stuck out like wind scoops, large yellow teeth and a Teddy Roosevelt grin. You expected the hearty manner, and out came this gentle, crooning voice.

"I'd gladly tune your piano," I told him. "But I didn't bring my tools."

"Ah, well," he said, "so much for Chopin. My dear cousin Geoffrey will just have to play Beethoven. Heaven knows, I tried. Here's a snifter of Rémy Martin. Coffee's on the fire. I hope you came to divulge *all* of the juicy details about last night."

"I'll give you what I know," I said. "And maybe you can give me some information from that encyclopedic brain of yours."

"Spare my blushes. I'll do what I can."

"Briefly, here's what happened. I surprised burglars in Alice's apartment last night, and I had to kill one of them. The other got away, but I've since determined that he's Count Carlo, the famous jewel designer. I figured you'd have the lowdown on him."

"I could write his book. Shall we make a tape?"

"Whatever you say."

"Let's go into my study."

I finished off my snifter and followed him into a slightly smaller room, one wall of which was a ceiling-high bank of white oak file cabinets. He went to his desk, by windows looking down to 43rd Street, and pressed a button on a small console.

"Okay," he said. "You first. Fill me in. How did you happen to surprise burglars in Alice's apartment? What were they looking for, and did they find it? Jewels were the

98

object, I take it, since Count Carlo was one of the burglars, which I find hard to believe . . . Well, on second thought, maybe . . . How do you know the man was Count Carlo?"

I related the story, step by step, beginning with Alice's mysterious disappearance during *The Cabinet of Doctor Caligari,* and ending with my visit to Carlo's shop on 57th Street. Not the whole story, of course, not the part about Herb Junep. For all I knew, Bubba might have turned born-again. Sometimes it takes awhile to show. He might feel righteous and call 911 like an honest citizen. Most people stop thinking when faced with violent crime, especially murder, and they feel impelled to *do* something. For openers they call the cops. This is all right when there's a chance of catching the murderer by prompt action, otherwise maybe not. Whoever knifed Junep was long gone. Why would he hang around? And there was no way of knowing whom to look for, man or woman, young or old, black or white. So far as I knew, there could have been more than one person involved in Junep's death. I mean besides Junep himself, of course.

When I'd finished I said, "Now, how about Carlo?"

"I'll get out his file," Bubba said. "But I have a lot of questions to ask you later."

His breakfast had arrived, and I insisted on waiting until he'd finished. Meanwhile I sipped black coffee. I felt like playing the piano, even Bubba's outraged Steinway, so I put down my cup and opened the piano lid. I stomped on the loud pedal and vamped some barrelhouse boogie, which sounds just fine on bad pianos. Bubba wolfed down his oatmeal with butter, honey, and cream, and when he'd finished he rang for the waiter.

Then he went to the wall cabinets and got out a manila file folder labeled "Carlo." He seated me at his desk and handed me the file. It contained a two-page biography and an assortment of newsclips.

Giovanni Batista Carlo was born in Rome in 1910, only child of a volcanologist and a coloratura from La Scala. They gave him a good education, and he got a liberal arts degree from the University of Rome in 1931. He was a Black Shirt by then, a youth leader. His talent for the design and fabrication of jewelry first showed itself when he was a child working with base metals and common stones like agate and obsidian. After the university he apprenticed himself to a Roman jeweler and managed to squirrel away enough of his employer's materials over a period of time so that he was able to make an original piece, which he sold for enough money to set himself up in a small way. The employer brought suit but could prove nothing, and besides he was not a member of any of Il Duce's organizations, being Jewish. He lost the case, whereupon Giovanni Batista Carlo sued him for libel, slander, and whatever the law allowed, and he won enough in compensatory damages to expand his small business considerably. It broke the Jew, but Carlo generously gave him employment, a stool and a bench, in his new, expanded shop, executing his, Carlo's, designs. I found nothing more about the Jew in the two-page bio. Carlo's success accelerated after his court victory. His baroque designs were much in demand. His price went up. Soon he opened a shop in Paris and began calling himself the Comte de Monte Carlo, at first in jest, but the name caught on and soon he was known everywhere as Count Carlo. In Rome he was a member of the Fascisti, in Paris of the fascist Croix de Feu. In 1939 he was called into Mussolini's army with the instant rank of lieutenant colonel. He served nobly in the daily campaigns of the Via Veneto, and with the help of his uniform, his rank, and his several decorations he conquered innumerable demi-mondes. After Il Duce's fall he buried his uniform and joined a special group of partisans under the command of an OSS colonel, John Patrick Pearse, from Boston. This group of *partigiani* came from all backgrounds, Anarchist, Communist, Socialist, Christian, Royalist, and ex-Fascists trying to make Brownie Points. But if they were not all anti-fascist, they were at least anti-Nazi and delighted to be harassing the German retreat.

After the war Carlo reopened his shops in Rome, Paris, and Hollywood in very high style, as if the war had been good for business. Now he moved his base to New York City, where he opened his present shop on 57th Street, becoming a U.S. citizen in 1958. In 1969 he did federal time for absconding with a large emerald on consignment from a midtown jeweler. He was released a few months later when he managed to produce the emerald. He claimed his tailor had filched it. The tailor claimed it had gotten lost in his button box. Since that time he had on occasion been suspected of fencing in a high-class way but had never been accused. His New York address was the Gainsborough.

When I'd finished, Bubba asked if I'd like to check the cross-index cards. He showed me to an oak table against a wall. On the table there was a small bank of card files like those in a public library.

I looked up Carlo and found many cards behind his, names of the rich and notorious, financiers and movie queens, politicians and oil sheikhs, mafiosi and army generals, most of whom had bought his jewelry. Among these clients and friends were four who interested me: the Principessa Francesca di Casoli, Charles Louis Urquhart, John Patrick Pearse, and Heinz Morgenlicht. The TV producer had bought a diamond solitaire ring for his wife. I mentally scratched his name from the list. According to the bio, Carlo had known Pearse in the war. And he'd designed a ruby ring for the principessa. So far, zilch.

I checked the principessa's index card and came up with three familiar names, for what they were worth, Count

Carlo, John Patrick Pearse, and Charles Louis Urquhart.

Well, what *were* they worth? I already knew about Carlo's and Urquhart's connection to the principessa. At any rate, I knew something about it, albeit not much. I asked Bubba for the file folder on Pearse. He got it out for me. Like Carlo's it had a two-page biography. Unlike Carlo's it had few newsclips.

John Patrick Pearse was born of poor parents, an Irish father and an Italian mother, in Boston, 1905. Grew up bilingual. Graduated West Point 1926, served in military intelligence until World War Two. When the Office of Strategic Services was formed he was chosen for his fluency in Italian and was sent in 1943 to work with a group of *partigiani* north of Rome. Retired as full colonel in 1946. In 1950 he bought four hundred acres of Glen Cove, millionaire country, and built a rambling stone villa, created a lake, a deer park, and the biggest aviary in the East. When not at his baronial estate he could be found at his sumptuous Manhattan pied-à-terre high in the Hotel Plaza with an unobstructed view over Central Park to Harlem and beyond, on a clear day.

How a retired army colonel had accumulated the capital for all this was a mystery. He was listed on some corporation boards, indicating that he did work, at least managing his money. He also traded in art. Newsclips named him as buyer or seller of some Cellini pieces, a collection of ancient Chinese jades, several Renaissance Italian paintings, Baroque garden sculpture, period furniture, notably a $140,000 Louis XIV secretary. He was not often seen at public affairs, and accordingly there were few photos of him. When seen at galleries he looked suave, debonair, and always had an elegant lady on his arm. Always a different lady. Lived alone except for servants. Generous contributor to the American Cancer Society, the Heart Fund, the Democratic Party, and other conservative causes.

The index cards had both Carlo's and Pearse's addresses and phone numbers. I wrote them down in my address book.

Then I asked for the principessa's file folder. According to Bubba's two-page bio, her title was as real as Carlo's was phony. It reached back to a bastard son of Alexander VI, the Borgia pope. Time confers legitimacy. Among the newsclips were several relating the Beverly Hills rape-murder and jewel robbery. Nothing new there except the detail that the Principessa Francesca di Casoli was the last scion of the name. There was also a newsclip that should have been duplicated, or at least noted, in Colonel John Patrick Pearse's folder, but wasn't. The item reported that she and Pearse had been the highest bidders at a Sotheby Parke Bernet auction last autumn. Carlota's Rosary had gone for $500,000 and the Spanish Dagger for $50,000. Both had gone to the principessa. The newsclip didn't mention Catherine's Egg, so I assumed she already owned it. The ruby ring, of course, would not have been up for auction, since it had been made expressly for her by Count Carlo, possibly not long before. I thought to try and check the date on that, but decided it could wait.

Nearly an hour had gone by since I phoned Morgenlicht, so I thanked Bubba and prepared to leave. I asked to use the phone and called Lieutenant Sweeney through Midtown North.

As soon as he came on the line he said, "Heard from the girl yet?"

I said, "Not yet."

"So what can I do for you?"

Bubba was nearby, fitting a queen-size cigarette into an 18-inch cigarette holder and frankly listening.

"I'd like you to run a name through that famous NYPD computer," I told Sweeney.

"What is it?"

"Moran, first name Terence, middle initial D."

"What about him?"

"Somebody who shall be nameless mentioned a Terence D. Moran in connection with a Charles Louis Urquhart."

"Yes? The world is waiting, Streeter."

"That's all. Maybe if we knew who Moran is we'd know more about Urquhart."

"I want to know who gave you the name."

"No kidding, Lieutenant, it's like I said, somebody who shall be nameless. It happens that I don't know the name. Just one of the Times Square characters. They call him Red. He has red hair. What could I tell you?"

"All right," Sweeney said. "Terence D. Moran is at present in Roosevelt Hospital with a stab wound in his chest, left pectoral muscle, not critical. Says he went into the ladies' room of a Hell's Kitchen saloon with a hooker and she hit him over the head from behind, and when he turned to face her she stabbed him. No robbery motive, he says, just one of your garden-variety Eighth Avenue whores. He was asked about a recently healed wound in his leg that looks like a bullet crease. He says he hurt himself rock climbing."

I said, "Which saloon?"

"Houlihan's. Know it?"

I did. It was at the corner of 50th Street and 9th Avenue, two blocks from Pal Joey's, and a low dive it was, with prosses turning tricks all over the place, cheap boosters peddling stolen trash, young hoods dealing deuces and trays of white garbage, and vice cops and narcs hanging around waiting for their grift.

I said, "What time was he stabbed?"

"Around two A.M."

"Thanks. I'll let you know."

"You'll let me know what, Streeter?"

"If there's a connection between Moran and Urquhart."

"And how will you discover that?"

"I don't know yet. Keep in touch. I'll call you."

I thanked him again and hung up.

"So who is this Terence D. Moran?" asked Bubba. "And why was he stabbed? That's all I could get from your end of the dialogue."

"He's a baddie," I said. "I don't know why he was stabbed, but it had to have something to do with the jewels. He may have been the one who shot Urquhart in the back."

"What are you going to do now?"

"First I'm going to view the videotapes of last night's show. I have a hunch Moran's in one of the crowd shots. Care to come along?"

"Absolutely! I expect an exclusive, you know."

11

It was two o'clock when we came out of the Algonquin, and I was already late for my appointment with Heinz Morgenlicht, so I grabbed a cab and we rode up the Avenue of the Americas to the television studios. Morgenlicht was waiting for me in the lobby. He was of course surprised to see Bubba Antrim with me.

"You know each other," I said. "I want Bubba to view the tapes with me. He was at the club last night. He may be able to help."

"It is always a pleasure to see Mr. Antrim," said Morgenlicht, letting his Berliner accent show a little and bowing stiffly from the hips. "I have arranged to have the viewing in my office." He led us toward the elevators. We took an express car to the fortieth floor. As we walked down a long, red-carpeted hallway, he said, "We shall have privacy, and perhaps you can explain to me what this is all about."

"It's not a secret," I told him. He was leading us through deserted outer offices toward his inner sanctum. "It seems there were three burglars last night. We've identified the one I killed. I believe the others may be in the crowd shots." A half truth is better than an out-and-out lie, right?

He unlocked his office, and we went into a vast space with windows on two sides, really an L-shaped window, and a view of Lower Manhattan and the harbor beyond. He pressed some buttons on his desk, and automatic blinds were drawn over the windows. The big room was bathed in soft light.

"They'll run the tapes in another room," he explained. "We'll receive them in here. If you want to study a shot, use this console."

The console was a small, remote control panel mounted on a dolly, with switches and knobs for stop-action and closeups, fast-forward and replay. We took chairs facing the screen, Morgenlicht and I on either side of the console, Bubba on my right.

Morgenlicht pressed a button, video and audio came on immediately with marvelous clarity, and we were looking at the opening of last night's show: first a shot of my hands on the keyboard, the camera moves back, and we see over my shoulder and through the upraised piano lid a young woman dancing and another singing "Sophisticated Lady."

I pressed the fast-forward button and held it until I saw the first crowd shot. Then I let the tape run at normal speed. I was looking, of course, for Charles Louis Urquhart, Count Carlo, or Terence D. Moran, whatever he looked like. I had a general description from his driver's license, but not the face, the man himself.

If I could put Moran on the club premises last night, it might help to explain a lot. I didn't expect to see him, or any of them, before *The Cabinet of Doctor Caligari* came on, for their interest in my show hardly extended beyond Alice. Every time the camera panned around the audience, picking up applause and laughter, singling out a celebrity, I watched for those three men. Though I studied every crowd shot, using the stop-action and closeup controls, I didn't see them.

The Cabinet of Doctor Caligari opened with a razzle-dazzle of Caligari's magical effects, *five* white rabbits hopping out of his top hat, *three* white doves flying out from under his opera cape, making a tour of the club, then coming to perch on his head and shoulders. He produced endless yards of colored silks, sudden clouds of red smoke, handsful of snakes that appeared and disappeared almost as fast as you saw them. I was in the background improvising from "Night on Bald Mountain" with a jazz beat. When Caligari had finished his opening, there was applause, and the camera panned around the club. My three suspects hadn't shown up yet. Then a pair of stagehands set up the cabinet.

Alice the cigarette girl came up from the audience. Unlike the traditional cigarette girl in nightclubs, with her Bunny costume, tutu, or whatnot, Alice dressed demurely in a long, austere Quiana gown, her hair braided atop her head in the style of the Tehuana women of southern Mexico. The way the Quiana draped itself on her body was sexier than Bunny costumes, tutus, and the rest. And, of course, she had The Look. Without even trying, she was sexuality incarnate. We weren't featuring sex in our entertainments at Pal Joey's, since every other door on Times Square opened into a topless joint, a peep show, or a porn movie. But naturally we did have some. When Stacy Brown sang "Rocks in My Bed Blues" with her sexy melding of Billie and Bessie, every man in the room stood, and every woman in the room knew it. When Alice the cigarette girl put down her tray and walked onstage, you could hear the crowd's quick intake of breath, a hushing sound. She had to do very little to get this reaction, simply walk naturally and look as if she felt the way she looked.

Caligari put her in the cabinet, closed the door, opened it after some abracadabra, and she had disappeared. More

108

magic, and she reappeared as Greta Garbo. Not a costume change, just the facial expression, bodily attitude, and of course the hair. During the applause the camera panned around. I saw a lot of people I knew, Lee Winograd, the play producer, and his current playwright, Sy Potter, composer Chips McCool, a press agent who called himself Frank Arthur, and the last of the great nightlife columnists, Bubba Antrim. He laughed like the country boy he was when he saw himself on the screen. I saw something that I hadn't noticed last night. Bubba was with someone who looked like Carmen Miranda in a pants suit, man's shirt and necktie, a boyish girlfriend, or vice versa. I glanced over at Bubba. His wrinkled red face was all smiles.

Alice disappeared again and reappeared as Marlene Dietrich. Applause. The camera panned. I spotted a very tall man among the SRO crowd at the bar. We had no stage lighting back there, so it was hard to be sure who the tall man was. I thought first of Urquhart, of course, and pressed the stop-action button, then turned the closeup control, but in the low light I still couldn't be sure. I released the tape and let it run. I thought the man had been bigger than Urquhart.

The camera moved back to Alice as Dietrich. The screen split. The camera moved in on Alice, keeping Caligari in long shot. I studied Alice's face and thought I detected a slight break in her impersonation. Dietrich's famous Look flickered, then held firm. Alice had the tight, steady concentration that makes great performers, keeps high-wire artists aloft, and gets laughs or tears on command.

Caligari closed the cabinet, did some hocus-pocus, and opened it again. Empty. He closed it, did some more mumbo-jumbo, opened it, and still no Alice. She should have been standing there as Marilyn Monroe. The rest of the impromptu script was familiar. She wasn't going to reappear. I waited for the next crowd shot. When the stagehands came and folded up the cabinet and took it off, the laugh came and the camera panned around the crowd.

The very tall man was no longer in the crowd at the bar. The camera covered the whole club, then returned to the piano, where I was vamping. I didn't seen the tall man again. I let the tape run to curtain, then switched it off, thanked Morgenlicht for his time and trouble, gave him a good cigar, and told him the viewing had unfortunately been fruitless. In fact I didn't know whether it had been or not. I had certainly seen a very tall man in the audience just before Alice's disappearance, and I was quite sure he was the one who'd spooked her. He could have been Charles Louis Urquhart, but I had a powerful hunch that he was Terence D. Moran . . . For a moment I saw how they could be one and the same: If Moran had worn colored contact lenses when he took his eye examination for the driver's license . . . Impossible. They could not be one and the same, because one of them was dead. And one was in Roosevelt Hospital. Putting it all together was too much for me. I thought perhaps I was trying to put it all together when I didn't have it all to put together. There were more sides to the problem than facets on a round-cut diamond. What problem? Keeping Alice from harm at the hands of a hood like Moran or a crook like Carlo, or a righteous man like Sweeney. And protecting her interests, which were mine.

We left Morgenlicht, and on the way down in the elevator I asked Bubba if he'd recognized anyone besides mutual acquaintances in the crowd shots. He thought about it. When we got to the lobby, he said no, he hadn't seen anyone I didn't know. Had he seen Count Carlo? No. What about John Patrick Pearse? No. I told him I was going to visit Count Carlo next. He wanted to go along, but I felt it would be wrong to let him, for I could see he wasn't dressed for the occasion. When we reached the street I headed

110

uptown toward Central Park South and the Gainsborough. Little old Bubba followed.

"You'll have to go home and get your piece first," I told him.

"What . . . ?" he said. "You mean a gun? I've never shot a gun in my life. I wouldn't know how. I've never even had one in my hand!" He looked up at me earnestly as we walked along. He was having a hard time keeping pace with me. He said, "You don't think Count Carlo would . . . ?"

"He cranked off three shots at me last night."

"But are *you* armed?"

"The word is *dressed,* and I can see you're not."

"Maybe I could sort of walk behind you?"

"You could front for me," I said.

"That's not funny. That's sick."

"What I mean is, if Carlo doesn't want to see me you could get us in."

"What kind of gun do you carry, Joey? I hope it's a big one. Do we have to walk so fast?"

I slowed the pace. The afternoon was getting on toward hot. We'd gone only two blocks, with five to go, which I could have walked in five minutes or less on a slow day, but Bubba was old and short in the legs. I hailed a Checker.

The Gainsborough is No. 222 Central Park South, about halfway between 7th Avenue and Columbus Circle. An elderly attendant manned an equally elderly elevator. No doorman, no guard. I thought it odd that a famous jewel designer would choose a building with so little security.

The attendant asked us whom we wished to see, and Bubba said, "Count Carlo. Tell him Bubba Antrim."

The attendant called upstairs on an old-fashioned intercom, announcing, "Two gentlemen to see you, sir, Mr. Bubba Antrim and a friend." He listened a moment, then said to me, "May I have your name, sir?"

"I'll talk to him," I said, and took the phone. "This is

Joseph Streeter. We'd like to come up for a few minutes, Count Carlo."

The ancient instrument crackled and sputtered. I could hardly make out what Carlo was saying. I thought he asked what I wanted to see him about. Then I thought, to hell with it, he and I were old buddies by now. Hadn't we exchanged shots already? Damn near a blood bond. I hung up the phone, nodded to the attendant, and stepped into the elevator, with old Bubba right behind me.

When we got off at the tenth floor I saw why the tenant had no need of security in the lobby. The elevator opened onto a foyer that had only one other door, a solid steel panel like a bank vault, with a heavily screened wide-angle lens where a judas hole would normally be. The elevator door closed behind us. I smelled carnations and remembered poison-gas drill at boot camp, but boot camp was long ago and I couldn't recall which gas smelled like carnations.

A man's voice said, "State your business, Mr. Streeter."

I looked for the loudspeaker and saw a small grill in a ceiling corner.

"It's about the Egg," I said. "What's that smell?"

"Incense," the voice said.

I heard a mechanical humming. The steel door slowly swung open. There was nobody in the doorway. I walked on through, with Bubba behind me, onto a balcony. The scent of carnations was much stronger now. About ten feet below and thirty feet away, standing by tall windows, Count Carlo was pointing a small automatic at me. I felt Bubba huddling close against my back. Beyond Carlo was the vast expanse of Central Park.

"That's a belly gun you're holding," I told him. "You'd need a lot of luck to hit me at this range, and you've just run out of luck."

He looked scared, but he held the gun pointing at me. He

was sweating. He wiped the back of his hand across his forehead.

Taking it slow and easy I opened my jacket, even more slowly drawing my P-38, but before I could take aim, Carlo had lowered his gun arm. I told him to drop the piece on the floor. He was looking into the black muzzle of my cannon. His eyes flickered away from it and into mine. I went down the stairway, slowly, with Bubba following close as my shadow. As we crossed the room, Carlo dropped his gun. I picked it up. It was a small Beholla, also known as the Menta, the Leonhardt, and the Stenda. It's a stopper only if you catch one of its 7.65mm slugs in a vital spot, but with only a 3-inch barrel, accuracy isn't one of the Menta's virtues. I offered it to Bubba, but he shook his head, horrified, and backed away from it. I dropped it in my pocket. If push came to shove and I had to involve Lieutenant Sweeney, the Menta would place Count Carlo in Alice's apartment last night. The fat little Roman was sweating harder now, breathing noisily, and trembling. His chins shook like vanilla junket. He made an eerie, whining sound.

"What are you going to do to me?" he whispered.

He looked ridiculous with his double-breasted blue-and-white seersucker suit, vest of blue watered silk with red buttons, two-tone blue-and-white suede pumps with red laces, white-on-white shirt and red-and-blue polka dot bow tie. Not over five feet four, not under two hundred pounds. The double chin had double chins. I patted him down. He felt like a giant Kewpie doll, but soft like new-risen bread dough. He carried no second gun.

We were standing by the windows, and I could see the bench in Central Park where I'd watched the dogs and the somersaulting squirrel and read the reviews only a short while ago.

"What am I going to do to you?" I said. "Well, first I'm going to ask you a question, Count. And then, if I don't like the answer, I'm going to drop you out of this window."

"*Gesucristo!*" he cried. "Maybe I don't *know* the answer!"

I said, "Let's find out." He fell to his knees. He clasped his hands tightly. He looked like he was going to cry. I holstered my gun so I could handle him better. I said, "Who has the Egg? Who has the Dagger?"

He almost shouted, "I don't know! I haven't got it! I swear on my mother's honor!"

I slapped him across the mouth and he fell over on his side. He raised his fingers to his fat lips, feeling for blood.

"Insult me with another lie," I said, "and I will defenestrate you quicker than you can say knife."

Lying on his side, with one leg bent under him, quivering like a giant jellyfish, he burst into laughter. It wasn't contagious laughter. It was hysterical. He laughed all over, shaking like a mound of aspic. He must have known the word *defenestrate.* The Italian *finestra* means window. Something about it tickled his funny bone. Maybe he'd never heard the English before. He got to his knees again, not laughing now but gasping like an asthmatic, and tried to crawl away from the windows. I kicked his arms out from under him, and he sprawled on the floor. He turned on his side and looked up at me with the big-eyed soulful appeal of a weeping iguana.

"Please!" he said. "Let me explain, Mr. Streeter. We found only the Spanish Dagger. You yourself put the Dagger into Charles. It was in him, I saw it, as I was leaving. How could I have taken it? And we didn't find the Egg."

I stepped on his neck and let him gag a little. Bubba put a hand on my arm, afraid I'd hurt the miserable coward. I eased up.

"You're lying again," I told Carlo. "You found more than the Spanish Dagger. What about the ruby ring?"

I stepped a little harder on his neck and let him gag some more. Bubba again tried to intercede. Carlo tried to pull my

114

foot off his neck but couldn't. When his face turned purple I eased up.

Gagging and gasping, he managed to whisper, "Yes, the ring . . . I forgot the ring . . . It is worth nothing. We found only the Dagger and the ring. Nothing else. Please, take your foot off my neck."

I reached down and grabbed him by the coat collar, dragged him protesting to the windows, and hoisted him up onto the sill. He flailed his arms about, trying to get loose, and he kept swearing he was telling the truth.

Bubba was dancing around us, pleading, "Joe! No! My God! Don't do it, Joe!"

When I had Count Carlo up on the windowsill, he yelled, "The truth! I am telling you the truth! Oh, God! Please!" I believed him now. He shouted, "Help! Help! Police!"

I doubted that the people on the street ten floors below could hear him. There were buses, taxis, and private cars on Central Park South by now. I pulled him inside the room again and dropped him to the floor. He hit the parquet with a soft thud. He was still shaking all over and sweating like a baby hippo, but he looked up at me with a tremulous smile, glad to be alive.

"Get up," I said. I reached down and helped him to his feet. He staggered over to a chair and fell into it, still weak with fear. "We'll talk," I told him. His clothes were a mess. He tried to straighten them. "If I retrieve the jewels," I said, "can you sell them?"

"But of course," he said. The prospect of doing business seemed to hearten him. "That has been my purpose all along, Mr. Streeter."

"There's quite a lot of money involved," I said. "I know the values. How long will it take you to make your arrangements?"

"I have a buyer waiting," he said. "My client desires to purchase all three pieces . . ." He cut himself short, as if

115

he'd said too much. He had. "Or whatever we can get," he added, "Catherine's Egg, the Spanish Dagger . . ." He seemed to consider, then added, "Carlota's Rosary?"

"That I can promise you," I told him. "The Rosary is in the bag. And now I know who has the Egg. So we can deal for those at least."

"You do not know who has the Dagger?"

"Frankly, no. Does it matter? It's value is only fifty thousand," I said. "I'll be content to deal for the Egg and the Rosary. They're combined value is four million."

"That is correct," Carlo said. "I can get you the usual ten percent, a nice four hundred thousand dollars. I hope that will be satisfactory?"

"Of course," I said.

"When can you produce the jewels?"

"I'll let you know."

"May I ask if the girl has the Rosary?"

"She's out of it, Count. She's in Atlantic City right now, enjoying a quiet vacation."

"Then who has it?"

"Terence D. Moran."

He looked the way he had when I held him over the ten-story drop to the street. His natural pallor seemed to pale further. He had trouble breathing.

In a small, choked voice he said, "Who?"

I said, "Good day, Count. Don't bother to show us out. As for the girl, if I hear of you coming within a mile of her I'll be back to finish what we started this afternoon. If anything happens to her, even if you're in Paris or Rome when it happens, I'll be coming to see you. Have a nice Fourth."

Bubba led the way up the balcony stairs, glad to be leaving. Count Carlo was looking out the windows and no doubt thinking about the sudden stop at the end of the long drop.

When we were on the balcony he turned away from the windows and called after me, "May I have my gun, please, Mr. Streeter?"

That's called chutzpah.

12

We stood in front of the Gainsborough looking up, half-expecting Count Carlo to drop a flower pot. I was thinking of Alice and wondering if she was lying low in my apartment as I'd advised her. Or had she disappeared again, into the wind, impersonating mad Empress Carlota Amalia trailing clouds of glory down Park Avenue . . . I couldn't call her, for I'd told her not to answer the phone. Or the doorbell. If the LAPD cops got there before I did, they might or might not ring the doorbell and wait, or come back later, but they were LA cops, after all, and just might crash in.

"What are you going to do now?" Bubba asked.

"Do you know Mister Magoo and Nickels Detroit?"

"No, but I knew Damon Runyon."

"He told it like it was," I said, "and it hasn't changed. Do you happen to know Hellfire Henry and Badfoot George?"

"Dear God, no."

"Well, I want someone to watch the Gainsborough while I run down to Times Square and get a couple of them to stake this joint out."

"Oh, dear."

"What's the matter?"

"He might come out while you're gone. What if he has another gun?"

"Here," I said. "Take his Menta."

"No! I'd rather die!"

"So wait in the park. You can stand among the bushes or behind a tree. If you see him come out, he won't see you. Follow him, and . . ."

"Joey! I really couldn't. I was so scared upstairs, I've been so scared all along . . ."

"All right," I said. "But will you wait until I send someone to replace you?"

"How will I know them?"

"You'll know them."

"Are you coming back?"

"No. When you're relieved, go to your hotel and wait for my call. You're going to get your exclusive, Bubba."

I waited until he'd entered the park and found a big tree to hide behind. He was peeking around it when I left. I found Hellfire Henry and Badfoot George still hard at work in Father Duffy's shadow. Thinking it over I realized that while George was right for the job I had in mind, staking out the Gainsborough discreetly, his partner might feel the urge to harangue the Central Park South gentry and this would draw heat. I didn't want to go up my own street just yet because of the fuzz around Pal Joey's, so I couldn't go to McAnn's and pick up Mister Magoo and Nichola Di uuli. They y'd almost certainly be there at this hour dealing their loose joints. I phoned McAnn's from the corner. Danny was behind the stick, afternoons, and he answered. I told him to send Magoo and Detroit down to the corner of Broadway. They came along in a couple of minutes, Detroit hobbling painfully and leaning on Magoo's shoulder. I told them what I wanted them to do and gave them each a double sawbuck.

"No word yet on Alice," said Detroit.

"She ain't holed up in none of the hotels," Magoo said. "Maybe she's up at this Gainsborough you sending us to, motherfucker."

"You can forget Alice. Just do this Gainsborough job, motherfucker."

Magoo grinned up at me and held out his hand. I slapped it. Then I hailed a taxi for them, put them in it, gave the driver a five-dollar bill and told him to keep the change.

"How do we get in touch with you?" Detroit asked.

"You phone me at home," I said. "If there's no answer, try again later."

I sent them on their way, then got out my address book and looked up the number I'd copied from Bubba's file card on John Patrick Pearse. There were two numbers, his pied-à-terre in the Hotel Plaza and his country home in Glen Cove. On a weekend, especially a long, noisy one like the Fourth, he'd most likely be out of town. I dialed 516 and the local number. A man answered. I said I was Joseph Streeter and asked to speak to Colonel Pearse. The man said he'd see if the colonel was in, which of course meant he *was* in, since the man would know if his master were out.

Another voice came on the line almost at once, saying, "This is Colonel Pearse. Do I know you, Mr. Streeter?"

"I'm the owner of a club called Pal Joey's."

"Of course! I've just now been reading about you in the paper. You must have had a rather stimulating night. What can I do for you, sir?"

"I'm calling about an auction," I said. "It was held last year at Sotheby Parke Bernet." I paused for a few beats, but Pearse didn't pick it up. "You bid on certain items, but you lost," I said. "I'd like to offer you the same items at a more accessible price."

120

"Accessible?" he said. "The price was accessible, sir. I was simply not interested beyond the price I bid. In any case, I'm no longer interested in purchasing those items. Sorry, but I'm afraid I can't help you."

"There's another matter to discuss," I said. "I'd like to meet you and talk it over."

"Perhaps," he said, "if you'll tell me what you wish to discuss . . . ?"

"The price of eggs," I said.

"Yes, of course," he said. "We'd better meet, the sooner the better. Since you know how to find me, perhaps you know my apartment in the city. I could be there . . ."

"The Plaza's too public," I told him. "I can be in Glen Cove within the hour. It's three-fifteen now."

"Unless you plan to fly," he said, "you'd better give it an hour and a half. Do you know Heliotrope Lane?" I said I did not. "It's very easy to miss," he said. "It turns off Glen Cove Road, to the right, about a quarter mile past Raynham Road. Do you follow?" I said I did. He said, "My gate-keeper will be expecting you."

I said, "That's me knocking on your door, Colonel."

I hung up, hailed a taxi, and told the driver to take me to 11th Avenue and 53rd Street, over by the docks. Buster's Bike Shop, garage and salesroom, was on the corner. It was a bright, sunny afternoon. All I needed was a helmet and jumpsuit, which I borrowed from Buster. He was a retired bike racer, having lost one eye in an accident. He'd looked like one of the Hell's Angels before. With the black eye patch he looked like Bluebeard. But he was a master mechanic and could tune a bike like a Stradivarius. He had all kinds of Hondas, Kawasakis, and some European jobs. I always rented a Harley. The Harley Davidson 1200 can't sprint like a Honda, being much heavier, but it has more power, rides like a flying featherbed, and can outrun any patrol on the road. When I was a kid in San Francisco, all

121

California highway patrols rode Harleys because they could catch most cars. The big Harley can still catch them, and leave them behind too, and does it better now.

I headed east on 59th Street intending to pause a moment on Central Park West and check with Detroit and Mister Magoo, but they weren't in the park where I'd told them they'd find Bubba Antrim. Neither was Bubba, of course. Then I spotted them moving slowly along the south side of the street toward 7th Avenue. I caught them at the corner. Detroit said they'd been on their way to a phone.

"Your man left the Gainsborough a few minutes ago," he said. "He got in a big black limousine, with a chauffeur, a rented job. Mr. Antrim described the man like you did, and he said if there was anything to report and you wasn't home we should call him. So we was on our way when you come along just now. Where you goin' on that motorcycle?"

"I'm going to catch up with that limousine," I said.

"Hoo-ee! You knowed he was goin' all along?"

"No, I didn't," I said. "But you need a little luck. Did you get the limo's license number?"

He told me the number, and he was right, it was a rental. I told them they could go on about their business, thanked them, and rode east, taking the Queensborough Bridge, not breaking any speed laws yet. Coming off the bridge on the Queens side I took Vandam Street to the Long Island Expressway, and when I hit the expressway I let her rip. I flew down the lanes, weaving among the cars like a hawk after a rabbit, so fast I nearly missed the rental limousine with the license number Detroit had told me. I caught a glimpse of Count Carlo in the back seat as I passed. He couldn't have recognized me because of the helmet and visor. I stepped on it a little, as the saying goes, though you don't step on it with a bike, you twist it. Anyhow, I got by with it until I was about ten miles short of my exit, and then a patrol car going the other way saw me.

I figured they'd get on the horn and there'd be a stakeout up ahead, and there was. The second car saw me coming half a mile away but got a bad start because of the traffic. I opened the Harley up. They radioed ahead, of course, and within a mile I picked up another patrol, but by now I was doing a hundred twenty and still climbing. It could have been fun, but I had to brake for Exit 39 North. The fuzz were so close behind me they couldn't brake soon enough to make the turn, and in fact they damn near ran me down when I squeezed the brake. They had to turn to miss me, and then they couldn't quite make the exit.

I took Glen Cove Road and kept well under the local speed limits, watching for my turn-off. Heliotrope Lane *was* easy to miss, a narrow opening between two weeping willows, with a small sign that was half obscured. The lane was a one-way road, hardly more than a twin-rutted track, with wide places from time to time for cars to pass. It wandered from Glen Cove Road around small hills and dells to the North Shore. The last driveway running off Heliotrope Lane had "Pearse" in wrought-iron letters over the gate. There was a gatehouse. A man in livery stood at the gate. He wore something heavy under his tunic by the left shoulder. I said I was Joseph Streeter, and he saluted and opened the gate.

"Just follow the drive," he said. "Better stay on your bike, though. We have dogs about."

Some of them came to greet me before I'd gone fifty yards. They were big German shepherds, three of them. The drive was lined on both sides with Lombardy poplars, and it wound past a small lake. There was a bit of an island in it, and on the island a fine, old-fashioned pergola. On the far edge of the lake stood an enormous glass-enclosed aviary, but I heard no birdsong though I had throttled down and was riding slowly. The shepherds kept pace, loping along on each side of me but at a distance from the bike.

Possibly they'd never heard the deep-throated rumble of a Harley. To tease them I revved the motor quickly, for just a second, and they closed in, barking furiously, but not close enough to nip me.

Pearse was standing at the top of broad flagstone steps leading up to the front porch of his villa. He put a whistle to his lips, and the dogs stopped their barking and stood ready for the next command. I cut the motor and lowered the kick stand. He remained on the top step until I'd taken off my helmet. Then he came down to meet me with his hand outstretched. He was my build, tall and lean, but at least twenty years older, though his hair was not as white as mine. He had a ready smile and an easy manner. We shook hands. He wore white flannels and a maroon smoking jacket with a patch: crossed tennis racquets.

He spoke to the three dogs and they came over, heads down, wagging their bushy tails and singing deep in their throats as shepherds do when they're glad to see you. They didn't know me, but their master had said it was all right. I knelt on the ground and let them come to me.

"You like dogs?" Pearse asked.

"Shepherds most of all," I said. "I owned one, a young female, silver-tipped. I called her Schatzi. She was killed by the same person who murdered my partner sixteen months ago. I still feel it."

"For your partner?" asked Pearse. "Or for Schatzi?"

I thought I'd made it clear, but he was looking at me rather oddly, the hint of a smile at the corners of his mouth and eyes. He looked the sort you could trust, a solid, healthy old man of the outdoors. His shepherds certainly trusted him. They were two bitches and a dog, and one of the females was silvery like my Schatzi. Now that he'd given them the key word, whatever it was, they treated me like a member of the family. So I wrestled them a little, letting them lick my face and gnaw the sleeves of my jumpsuit.

When I stood up, the shepherds stood up too, their big paws on my chest, wanting to play some more.

Pearse laughed and said, "I'll have to get some new dogs, I'm afraid. They're supposed to guard the property, not welcome strangers with kisses. You must have a special charm." But we both knew they'd have bitten my head off if he hadn't been standing there. He said, "Giorgio! Zia! Nana!" They suddenly left me and sat on their haunches, watching him, waiting for orders. "Come in," he said to me. "I was about to prepare martinis. I hope you'll stay for dinner?"

"No, thanks very much," I said. "But I'll have a drink with you."

Following him into the house I noticed that the left pocket of his smoking jacket hung low. There was something heavier than a briar pipe in it. When he'd closed the door behind us, he put an arm lightly around my shoulders and ushered me into a large reception room. He managed to touch me under the left arm as he did this. I didn't mind. What's fair is fair. Now we both knew. But I wouldn't have thought he'd have to do more than look, for the P-38 was never designed for concealment in a shoulder holster.

Pearse lived in the grand style. The villa was a rambling stone house, two wings extending from the central reception room. The walls of this room were decorated in heavy white silk, and the furnishings were in the style of Louis XV, with rare plants growing out of lacquered boxes, hand-carved rosewood furniture, sofas covered in Beauvais tapestry, Venetian mirrors, shelves of morocco-bound books, a gilded antique clock decorated with porcelain birds. He also had a Pleyel piano. I wanted to try it, but time was pressing.

"Martinis?" he asked. I nodded. "I use Bombay gin," he said. He began the ritual. As he prepared, we talked. "You said something about the price of eggs . . . ?"

"Yes, but I want to unload the whole boodle."

"I suppose I could handle it for you . . ."

"What you do is your business, Colonel. What I want is a straight deal. I'm selling, to you or to somebody else. It's a straight sale. You can handle later."

"May I assume you have actual possession of the merchandise?"

"Of course."

"Then I'm prepared to offer you the usual ten percent," he said. I said nothing. He got the idea. "But in matters of this kind," he said, "ten percent is the customary arrangement."

"It's not customary with me, Colonel."

"Then tell me what you want, sir. A finder's fee?" He handed me a martini. "Did you expect a reward of some kind, sir?"

He was being deliberately obtuse, of course, and stalling me.

"Fifty percent of list price," I said.

"Impossible!"

"Lloyd's would pay it rather than have to pay full value to the principessa's estate."

"Would you consider twenty-five? I can offer you certain advantages, a clean deal, no risk of entanglements with the law, and only you and I need ever know that the popular jazz pianist and owner of Pal Joey's . . ."

"Forget it," I told him. "I said a straight deal, not a clean one. There's no way to clean up this deal. And I'm not worried about entanglements with the law. You're not talking to a schoolboy, Colonel. Hot rocks are nothing new in my life. I started Pal Joey's with a bag of Brazilian diamonds so hot they smoked. I hijacked them from some thieves who'd ripped off a mine owner, who'd been ripping off his *mestiço* slaves for a long, long time, and that's an old, old story. So I don't know what you mean by a clean deal.

126

Money deals are never clean. But they *can* be straight. You make a fine martini."

"Thank you, sir. Let me freshen your drink."

I offered him a Brazilian cigar. He took it. We lit up.

"Fifty percent would be over two million," he said, "if I take all three pieces. It would take time to get that much cash together. Can you at least wait until the banks open? Monday's the Fourth. Say, Tuesday . . . ?"

I agreed, for what it was worth. And now, if I had him figured, he'd ask to see the merchandise before withdrawing or borrowing over two million dollars cash. He approached the question obliquely.

"I wonder if you know how these big jewelry deals are handled, sir?"

"No," I said. "And it doesn't matter to me how they're handled, Colonel. Only the bottom line, as they say."

"But there are certain difficulties," he said, "certain formalities. One rarely uses cash, sir, whether currency or checks, for the whole amount of the purchase. Financing is arranged with one's bankers, notes are signed. Very little cash is required, but a lot of credit. How good is my credit with you, sir?"

"Carry on, Colonel. I'm listening."

"You see, sir, I'm taking you on faith when you say that you actually have possession of the merchandise, Catherine's Egg . . ."

"And Carlota's Rosary. And the Spanish Dagger."

"Yes, well, I'm really only interested in the Egg,"

"It's a package," I said. "All or nothing at all."

"If you insist," he said. "But I should like to *see* something, the pieces, or at least proof . . ."

"You can view all three tomorrow night," I said.

"Very good, sir. Then I shall go to my bank the following day. But we could expedite our deal if I could view them tonight instead."

"Sorry," I said. "There are still detectives in my building, in the club and probably upstairs. They should be gone by tomorrow night. If they're not, I'll phone you in plenty of time."

"We could use my suite at the Plaza."

"Good of you to offer," I said. "But I'd rather do it on my premises."

"You're a careful man, sir. I like that."

"A careful man wouldn't be here, Colonel."

"At least you're honest."

Malarkey, I thought. But I didn't correct him. Why should I? He didn't believe it.

"You could give martini lessons to my barman," I said. He started to refill my glass. I put my hand over it. "It's dynamite," I said. "And I'm flying on only two wheels, remember."

"Yes, I was wondering how you expected to get out here from midtown in less than an hour. Well, when shall I come tomorrow night?"

"I think about nine," I said. "Make it nine-thirty, unless I call you."

"Sure you won't have another before you go?"

"One of your Bombay martinis should be enough for anyone," I said. "I've had two."

He walked me to the front steps. The dogs were somewhere on patrol.

"You must come again," he said, "when it's not on business. I'd like to show you through the house. Aside from dealing in art, I have a small collection that is permanent. Are you interested in antiques, Mr. Streeter?"

"You have some Louis XV pieces in your reception room," I said.

"Very good, sir," he said. "Very good, indeed. I see you know your jewelry *and* your antiques." We were standing at the top of the wide flagstone steps leading down to the drive. "And I should like to show you around the grounds," he said. "Do you see the round-topped glass roofs above the trees over there? That's my aviary. Are you a bird lover, Mr. Streeter?"

"I like animals," I said. "I noticed your aviary as I drove around the lake."

"Most men care little for our feathered friends," he said. "Women appreciate my aviary more. I had it designed by Mahmoud Kizilkayas, the Turkish architect. It's a technical marvel, with several sections, each with a different habitat, controlled environments according to the needs of the various species. It isn't a complete aviary. I have no penguins. But I do have an eagle, just one, a male bald eagle. I've been trying to buy a female, but they're very hard to get, being an endangered species. There's an eagle-feather merchant out in Colorado who keeps promising. I send him money, he sends me promises. But what can one do? He did get me the male. Have you just a few minutes, Mr. Streeter? I'd like you to see him. He's fierce. I call him Emperor. What a beauty!"

For a second, or less, I had a wild urge to take him up on it, shoot the glass walls out of the giant aviary, and liberate the eagle. But bald eagles have a survival problem on Long Island. Trigger-happy shooters use them for target practise.

"Some other time," I said. I thanked him for his hospitality and put on my helmet. "Nine-thirty, Monday night," I reminded him. "We'll meet in the club. You'll be my guest. I'll have my chef prepare something special, or perhaps I'll prepare it myself."

"You cook too? A veritable Renaissance man!"

What is it about the Irish? I revved the motor so I wouldn't have to hear more. The American eagle found a friend that day. As I scattered the gravel of the colonel's driveway I resolved to do something for Emperor.

The shepherds heard the motor and caught up with me as I was passing the lake, and they kept pace, barking but not angrily, all the way to the gate. The gatekeeper heard me coming and had the gate open. As I flashed on through I looked back and saw the three shepherds at the gate watching me go. It was time I found another Schatzi. As soon as this jewel scam was over . . .

Rounding a turn about halfway along Heliotrope Lane on my way to Glen Cove Road, a limousine with familiar rental plates ran off the narrow road and into the bushes on seeing me suddenly looming upon them. There was no need, for I wouldn't head-on while riding a Harley. Not even a Harley.

Just in case the highway patrols were thinking I might come back, I avoided the Long Island Expressway and took Northern State to the Cross Island to the Belt, then around through the Brooklyn-Battery Tunnel to Lower Manhattan and up the West Side to Hell's Kitchen and Buster's Bike Shop. It was five-fifteen. The round trip, including my thirty minutes or so with Pearse, had taken exactly two hours, and I'd only been chased once on the way back. Hardly worth mentioning. He gave up after the first mile. No guts.

So it shouldn't be a total loss, what had I learned by running out to Heliotrope Lane? That Col. John Patrick Pearse did not have Catherine's Egg? Not necessarily. He was Irish and a master of the blarney. And crooked as a bulldog's hind leg. As Balzac said, behind every great fortune there is a crime. Colonels don't get rich on retirement pay. Did he want the Egg? No doubt. Would he pay fifty percent of book value, over four million, cash? Much doubt.

As I walked from the bike shop down to 50th Street and over to the club, I enjoyed wondering about the confrontation between Colonel Pearse and Count Carlo. That bit of dialogue must have been pretty funny, what with the count telling the colonel how I'd held him over ten stories of empty air trying to force him to tell where the Egg was, and the colonel telling the count how I'd claimed to have possession of the Egg *and* the other items. Or would they tell so much? No, more likely they'd hold out on one another, exchange a lot of lies, and part, convinced of each other's mendacity. But would Colonel Pearse come to the club tomorrow night? I thought he would.

13

There were a lot of city cars now in my block. I wondered if Junep's body had been found. When I went in I saw the LA detectives had arrived. They were swarming all over the joint.

Stacy and Colleen were onstage, but not rehearsing now. Three detectives were interrogating them, and the girls were furious. When they saw me they started yelling.

Stacy yelled at me first, "We're quitting this goddamn nut house! How can we work with all these clowns kibitzing?"

Then Colleen yelled at me, "What are you running here, Joe, a police precinct or a nightclub?" One of the cops started to say something to them, and Colleen took a short step toward him, kicked high, and knocked off his hat without touching his head. She danced away, saying, "Sorry, Officer. We're *working* around here!"

Two of the detectives headed toward me, one of them pointing a big cigar at me and saying, "Who are *you*, mister?"

Lieutenant Sweeney appeared from the corner by the back end of the bar and said, "This gentleman is Mr. Joseph Streeter, proprietor of the club. He's the one who surprised the burglars upstairs and killed one of them. Took the knife away from him and then gave it back to him." He laughed at his joke. Though the stabbing of Urquhart hadn't been preying on my mind the last few hours, I still didn't think it was funny. "Mr. Streeter," he said, "meet Detective Lieutenant Tom Snead of the LAPD."

"Pleased to meet you," Snead said. "Would you mind going over it for me, Mr. Streeter?"

"Yes," I said. "I would."

"Good. Now, if you'll just begin at the beginning, when you first discovered the burglars . . ."

"What Mr. Streeter means," Sweeney explained, "is that he does mind. He doesn't want to go over it again. I for one don't blame him. I have his statement on file."

"Well, I understand how you feel, too, Mr. Streeter, but on the other hand," Snead said, "if you'll just go over it for me, step by step, leaving out the bad parts, you know, the parts that upset you, okay? Maybe I'll see something that Lieutenant Sweeney overlooked. It's possible, you know." He grinned at Sweeney, who didn't grin back. "Well, you know," Snead said, "nobody's perfect."

"Lieutenant Sweeney is," I said. "Now if you don't mind, I'm going up to my apartment and get some rest. I haven't slept since . . ." I managed a choking sound, coughed lightly, took out my pocket handkerchief and dabbed my lips, I wiped imaginary sweat from my forehead. Alice would have been proud of me. "Please," I said. "Perhaps later."

And I walked quickly away. In the backbar mirror I could see Sweeney grinning at the LA detective's back. I caught his eye, and he winked. It helps to have a friend in the right places.

There were more LA dicks on the stairway, and they asked me to identify myself. I did so. They tried to interrogate me. I told them to see Lieutenant Sweeney. They could read my official statement. They got pushy. I pushed past them.

As I was unlocking my door, one of them said, "You live in there?" I said I did. "You have the whole floor?"

"That's right."

"Mind if we come in and look around?"

"Of course I mind. My apartment is not involved in this investigation. The burglary and homicide happened upstairs. You know where. If you have any questions, see Lieutenant Sweeney."

I went in and triple-locked the door. The phone rang. I picked it up at the living room bar. It was himself.

I told him to come on up, then went into the bedroom. Alice wasn't there. I found her in the bathroom, taking a bath, and told her to stay put, Sweeney was coming up. I leaned down and kissed her, grabbed a feel, and kissed her again. With enormous willpower, I wrenched myself away, went out with only one long look back, and closed the bathroom door feeling like a pillar of salt. I also closed the bedroom door, and locked it. Sweeney was ringing the doorbell.

There were some LA cops in the hall behind him when I opened. As I let him in, they tried to peer past him into the apartment. I triple-locked the door again and took Sweeney to the bar.

"What'll it be? You look better. Get some rest?"

"Whatever you're drinking," he said. "No, I just took a pill."

"Prescription?"

"My wife's. Why?"

"It's a federal violation."

"Quit kidding, Streeter. These boys from LA . . . And

134

that isn't the half of it. Internal Affairs . . . What are we drinking, Streeter?"

"Cognac?"

"Fine."

I poured two big ones and set up two glasses of ice water. We drank.

"What's with Internal Affairs?" I asked.

"They're worse than the Gestapo," he said. "A gang of paranoid maniacs . . . You won't believe this, old buddy, but they see coincidences between what happened here last year and what happened last night. And what are the coincidences? You well may ask. They are you and me and Pal Joey's. They smell a conspiracy. A conspiracy to do what, they aren't prepared to say, but they point out that there have been two homicides on the premises, and *you* have been involved in both. What's worse, *I* drew the job each time. They did some investigating, and they suspect you were more involved in last year's homicide than you appeared to be at the time. They wonder what you're up to this time. They think I ought to be able to tell them."

"Are you trying to ask me something, old buddy?"

"You might put it that way."

"Are you really worried about Internal Affairs?"

"Like death and taxes," he said.

"Would it help if you collared the cop killer those LA detectives are after?"

"I'd have to know *how* I collared him," Sweeney said. "Not like last time . . ."

"How do you like Terence D. Moran?"

"Why him?"

"I don't know yet."

"But you know *something*, Streeter, or you couldn't say what you did. Now God damn it, *I* want to know what *you* know!"

"You already know everything I know," I said. "When I know more, I'll let you know."

"Damn it, Streeter! I could take you down!"

"Do that, and I won't be able to help."

Sweeney drank his cognac, all of it. I poured him another double. He drank some of his ice water.

"What do you want me to do?" he asked.

"Do nothing," I said. "You say Moran wasn't hurt seriously. Then he'll be coming out of the hospital soon. That's when I'll give him to you."

"Oh, no! I'm not letting you run my case, Streeter. You must be out of your tree."

"Then what *will* you do, old buddy?"

"Never mind what I'll do. If *you* do anything I'll put you in a cage. Get that, Streeter!"

"All right, then," I said. "But if you tap his hospital phone, try not to let him know it. And if you tail him when he leaves Roosevelt, try not to use a cop who looks like a cop. That'll be tough, because nowadays cops look like everybody else . . ."

"Streeter!"

"I didn't mean you, old buddy. You look like what you are."

"Tell me the name of this game, Streeter. Maybe I could play too."

"I don't know the name of this one, old buddy. When I do, I'll deal you in. One thing I can tell you, if you let Moran come to me, without scaring him away with wiretaps and flatfeet, you'll collar the cop killer and maybe a couple of other perpetrators too."

"Tell me what you know, and maybe I'll cooperate."

"Trust me. Remember, and trust me."

"If word of this got out . . ."

"Why should it? How could it?"

"Internal Affairs would love it, Streeter. They'd get *you*

136

for obstructing. They'd get *me* for sheer incompetence."

"When will these LA cops be gone?" I asked.

"By tomorrow, I hope."

"I need to know."

"By tomorrow for sure."

"Then tomorrow night you get your cop killer if he can leave the hospital. I'll give you plenty of notice."

"I wish you'd tell me what you know."

"I wish I could. If I did, you'd have to do certain things, and that would end the story. You'd never make the collar. But *I* don't have to react like a cop, do I? Not being a sworn officer of the law. Just try to keep those LA dicks away from me. I'll do the rest."

"They've been trying to get into your apartment. They can't without proper authority, of course, and they want me to get a warrant."

"So what do they expect to find in here?"

"They spotted something we missed, jimmy marks on your windowsill. I had to pretend I knew all about it. I told them you locked yourself out one time, had to break in to your own place. But they don't like the way you nailed those windows shut. They can see why you nailed the one jimmied window shut, but they can't see why you nailed the other one shut too—that is, if you did in fact break in yourself, as I told them . . . See what I mean, Streeter?"

"I see that you don't lie too good, old buddy. But thanks for trying."

"Do I get a little reward, Streeter? Like who jimmied your rear window?"

"Would you believe, I don't know?"

"When did it happen?"

"Weeks and weeks ago."

"They don't look much weathered."

"What?"

"The jimmy marks," he said, "on the windowsill."

137

"The sills are hardwood."

"You should have reported a break-in, you know. Not reporting a felony is an infraction itself. Was anything stolen?"

"No. That's why I didn't report it."

"Incidentally, where did you fly off to this afternoon?"

"When I'm uptight," I said, "I often rent a bike and just go. The speed and the wind refresh my mind. How come you had me tailed?"

"Because I remember," Sweeney said. "And I see it happening again."

"Of course," I said. "I told you, old buddy, you'll get the collar, maybe more than one."

"Dead or alive?"

"Alive, I hope."

"I'm getting a headache, Streeter. The harder I try to trust you, the harder my head hurts."

"Have some more brandy." I hit him again, a big one, myself too. I gave him a cigar, held the match for him. When he had a good coal going, I said, "Lieutenant, let me level with you." He looked expectant. "You're a good cop," I said. "And you're a smart detective. But sometimes you can't be both, and this is one of those times. There's no way you can close this case and remain a good cop. A smart detective, maybe, if you got by with what you'd have to do."

"I see what you're driving at," he said. "You know, *you* could get in trouble, maybe very serious . . ."

"I'm already in trouble," I told him, "up to my ears if I don't handle it right."

"Why can't you tell me about it?"

"Because it involves other persons."

"Who?"

"I can't tell you that."

"I've been wondering if you're not trying to protect

somebody. Who is it? The girl, Alice what's-her-name?"

"Would it be a crime to try and protect my woman?"

"It might, Streeter, it might. Funny thing about her, not only doesn't Immigrations have a record of her—and you said she was born in Mexico, right?—but you also said she went to UCLA, and they don't have a record of this María de los Angeles et cetera. You make anything out of it?"

"Theater people tend to do that a lot," I said. "They'll credit themselves with roles they only tried out for, reviews that had only one good word in five hundred, triumphs that never happened except in the theater of their minds. But it isn't their alleged credits that count, it's what they do when you put them on a stage. I never checked Alice's credits or anything else about her background, and I couldn't care less. When she gets up there, what happened or didn't happen at UCLA means nothing. How a queen achieves her crown is a small matter. It's how she wears it."

"Streeter, are you drunk?"

"Certainly not," I said, realizing suddenly that I was. So was Sweeney. "Why do you ask?"

"I never heard you talk that way before. I believe you told me once that you left home when you were twelve. Did you go to school later?"

"I've always read a lot. Besides, I've spent my life playing piano in various parts of the world, and a lot in this country, and I've known all kinds of people, learned languages, different customs . . ."

"You say you read a lot? I don't see any books here."

"They're in my study."

"A study too, eh? Would you mind showing me around?"

"Now?"

"If you don't mind."

"Well, if you like."

"It's a fine place you have here, Streeter." He did a small take. "Oh, I hope you don't think I'm snooping?"

He was drunk. But how drunk? He was handling. How drunk did he think I was? And I was. Buddies we might be, but Sweeney was a snoop, drunk or sober.

"Come along," I said. "That door leads to the master bedroom. We'll go this other way."

I led him toward the rear of the apartment. First I showed him the guest room, which he could see at a glance was unoccupied. In the study he commented on my reference works, histories, encyclopedias, dictionaries, gazeteers, and so forth. In the back parlor he admired my instruments, the Melodean with its needlepoint-covered bench, the eighteenth-century square piano, the harpsichord, and my prize, the joy of my heart, a Beckstein baby grand of hand-carved hardwood, enameled ivory, and decorated with cherubs and gilt. Just right for an eighteenth-century cat-house. He also admired the back porch and the garden below. I observed that he took note of the fire escape and the stairs descending to the garden.

"Whoever jimmied your window," he said, "could have come up from the garden or down from the roof, or one of the upper floors. You say the break-in happened some weeks ago. I think you don't want to talk about it. I think it happened after last night's burglary, and the burglar who got away came back to look in your place for something he didn't find upstairs. That's what I think, Streeter, and I also think you know what he was looking for. Jewelry, right?"

"I'll tell you the truth," I said, and I did. "I don't think a burglar jimmied that window."

"Streeter, you're drunk."

"You noticed."

"I'd best be going now. Thanks for the refreshment. Could I have another one of those fine Brazilian cigars before I go?" I gave him one. He bit off the tip and spat the shreds on the floor. Now I knew how drunk he really was, for not even Sweeney, abrasive as he could be, would spit

140

on his host's floor, unless drunk. As I held the match for him, he stared into my eyes as if searching my mind. We stood eyeball to eyeball until the flame burned my fingers. I dropped it on the floor and stepped on it. "Keep me informed," he said, and headed for the wrong door, the master bedroom door. I directed him to the hall door. As he went out, he said, "Don't forget."

I locked up and went into the bedroom. A track of wet footprints in the dust on the bedroom floor led from the bathroom to the living room door. I stared at them, wondering why they led in only one direction, until I realized that if Alice had spent much time eavesdropping at the door, her feet would have dried before she went back to the bathroom. I studied the floor closely. A second set of tracks was barely visible, leading back to the bathroom. I went in to her. She was in the tub, up to her cute little chin in bubbles.

"Learn anything?" I asked. She smiled up at me, giving me her best Monroe baby stare. "The apartment needs dusting," I explained. "The floors take wet footprints very clearly."

"Oh, that!" she said. "I was just curious. You keep everything so secret, Joey. Is it because I'm a woman and you don't let women know what you're doing, like those sickies in *The Godfather?*"

"One question deserves another, I know, sweetheart. Me first."

"Men!" She rose out of the bubbles just a little, just enough. Fascinating. "Did I learn anything," she said. "Well, let's see. I learned that you went for a bike ride this afternoon. And Lieutenant Sweeney is having you tailed." She was ticking off the points on her fingers. "I also learned that you were involved in a homicide last year, that this mysterious Moran is a cop killer, that Internal Affairs is after Sweeney for something, that someone jimmied one of

141

your porch windows . . . How'm I doin', Teach?" Her Marilyn Monroe impersonation was always a turn-on for me. There was really no point in talking further. I knew all I had to know. I took off my clothes. "Oh, goody!" Alice cried, clapping her hands. "I guess I did all right, huh, Teach?"

I designed the bathroom myself, bought large-size fixtures, a big, old-fashioned john with overhead water box and chain, a walk-in shower roomy enough for a chorus line, and an Olympic tub for water sports. When we climbed out of the tub at long last, we were limp as noodles. We went straight to bed for a late siesta, and Alice fell at once into a light sleep. I couldn't turn off my mind. So I got up without disturbing her and went to my study and shut and locked the door.

I looked up Roosevelt Hospital in the book and dialed the number for patient information. When I asked about Terence D. Moran's condition, the operator had me wait a moment, then said Mr. Moran's condition was good, and did I wish to speak with him? I said I did. I heard her ring his room.

A grumpy baritone said, "Hello."

I said, "Mr. Moran?"

"Who's this?"

"Joseph Streeter."

"Who'd you say?"

"Joe Streeter, the owner of Pal Joey's."

"I dunno. Who?"

"I'm the piano player at Pal Joey's, where you were last night, or didn't you notice?"

"Oh, yeah. So what can I do for you, Mr. Streeter?"

"How are you feeling?"

"Lousy. Why?"

"When are you being discharged?"

"What you wanta know that for?"

142

"I think we should meet. We can talk about the Egg."

"*You* got it?"

"No, but I know who has."

"So what you want with me?"

"I could use your help in retrieving it, first, and then perhaps in selling it. I hear you've got connections."

"Oh, yeah? What are you, a cop?"

"How could I be a cop, Moran? Think it over."

"Yeah. Right. Okay, so when you wanta do this? I get outa here tomorrow sometime, if I'm all right, they tell me. Hell, I'm gettin' outa here tomorrow whether they like it or not. It's like bein' in the joint, this dump."

"Get out of there now," I told him. "Listen to me, Moran. Hear me good. Get out of there and get out of sight. Stay off the street until tomorrow night. Come to Pal Joey's at nine-thirty. Don't be early, and don't be late. Got it?"

"Do we do it tomorrow night?"

"We do."

"Okay, Streeter. Nine-thirty."

Sweeney had only my word on Moran, not enough to bust him, so I figured he'd play it safe, let him run loose but hang a tail on him. He'd taken the bait, and if he didn't spot Sweeney's surveillance he'd come. Armed, of course, and ready to shoot first.

I went back to the bedroom. It was six-thirty. Alice was snoring softly, a small whuffling sound. I leaned over the bed and kissed one bare breast. The whuffling ceased. She was so lovely lying there with her chestnut hair spread out upon the pillow like a mane in the wind. I got into bed and took her in my arms and kissed her again. She awoke and reached for me, pulling me on top of her. I felt like a Judas.

14

Later that evening we prepared dinner together and talked about the future. She wanted to do more improvisation, like *The Premise* when it first played in the Village, and I agreed, she had marvelous facility at improvisation. She could teach Stacy and Colleen, Caligari and . . . I said we'd have to find a comic to replace Herb Junep. She didn't react. Or she did. Sometimes reaction is best improvised as an appearance of no reaction. It used to be called underacting.

After dinner we watched some TV for a while, but there was so much patriotic gore on all channels, what with this July the Fourth weekend, that we gave up on it. We went into the back parlor, and I played the piano. No good. I couldn't think of any but sad songs. I tried Alphonse Picou's once famous riff from "High Society," but my heart wasn't in it. So we ended up in the front parlor at the bar.

Then I remembered the reviews that I'd torn out of the newspapers, and I gave them to Alice. She was as pleased as a child with a Christmas toy. And rightly, too, for every reviewer singled her out for special praise, all said she was headed for a great career. The irony would have depressed me but for the booze.

There was no reason to delay longer, so I told her I thought I had a buyer for Carlota's Rosary."

"Oh, Joey!" she cried. "So soon? How did you do it?"

"Magic."

"Come *on*, Joey! Don't tease."

"Listen to this," I said. Using the bar phone extension I dialed Count Carlo's apartment in the Gainsborough. He answered. I said it was Joseph Streeter calling. He made a noise like a cat gagging on a fishbone. "Would you like to view the merchandise," I asked him, "say tomorrow night?"

"I don't trust you, Mr. Streeter," he said. "Was that you on the motorcycle this afternoon?"

"That it was, Count."

"Why did you go to the colonel?"

"Just shopping around," I said.

"Is it true that you offered him all three items?"

"It's true, but not for ten percent, Count. What else did he tell you?"

"He said he refused."

"He did?"

"Is that all you have to say, Mr. Streeter?"

"Can you come to Pal Joey's at nine-thirty tomorrow night?"

"To view the merchandise?"

"Y . "

"When you were at my apartment this afternoon, you did not have one of the items, as I recall. You were quite insistent about that point. An hour later you offered all three items to Colonel Pearse. You see, I am sure, why I do not trust you, Mr. Streeter."

"The situation has changed," I said.

"Rather quickly," he commented. "But I shall come."

"Nine-thirty sharp," I said. "Don't be early, and don't be late."

As I hung up, Alice said, "Was that Count Carlo?"

"He's the buyer," I said.

"For the Rosary?"

"Yes."

"How much will he pay?"

"Full value," I said.

"A half million? The whole price? Oh, Joey!"

"You said I should only sell the Rosary, right?"

"Yes. I don't have the other . . ."

"Well, I have another buyer who'll take everything, Catherine's Egg, Carlota's Rosary, and the Spanish Dagger. Full value. He's prepared to pay cash on Tuesday, when the banks open. We could deal for the Rosary alone, tomorrow night with Count Carlo, or we could . . ."

"But I don't have the other things, Joey! You said Count Carlo found the Egg when he and Charles robbed my apartment . . ."

"No, I didn't say that, sweetheart. I might have said it *looked* that way. No matter. It's up to you."

"We'll take the money for the Rosary," she said. "And we'll go away for a while, until all this trouble is over."

"All this trouble," I thought, was a bizarre way to refer to homicide. Not to mention mendacity.

"Sure," I said.

"Where shall we go, love?"

"Coney Island?"

"Be serious, Joey."

"I am, sweetheart. Tomorrow's the Fourth, so we go to Coney, okay?"

"Okay! I haven't been in years. But the parachute drop is closed."

"But the Cyclone is open! We'll buy a whole string of tickets. And firecrackers!"

"I *love* the Cyclone! And the Wonder Wheel!"

Everyone has his dream world. I'd touched hers, Coney Island. It was better than Disneyland. So it was settled, we'd go out to Coney tomorrow and spend the Fourth on the rides. Maybe we'd go swimming.

Later in the night, when she was sleeping soundly, I went into my study and phoned Colonel Pearse. His man gave me a little static about the late hour and the colonel having retired, so I left the word: Viewing at Pal Joey's, nine-thirty sharp, Monday night. He should phone if he couldn't make it.

I sat in the study for a long time after that, thinking grisly thoughts. Herb Junep was lying stiff upstairs in a tub of cold red water. My lover lay sleeping in my bed. I got out a bottle of John Jameson and poured three fingers in a water tumbler. I lit a cigar and smoked and sipped for a while.

Then I phoned the greenroom. I let it ring a lot, then looked up Matt's lady friend's number. I dialed it. She answered, sleepy but good-natured, and when I told her it was I, she nudged Matt awake. It took him a minute to clear his head.

I told him I wanted him to be at the door as usual tomorrow night at nine-fifteen. Guests were coming at nine-thirty. I described them: fat little Count Carlo, tall Terence Moran, elderly, distinguished-looking Colonel Pearse, and Bubba Antrim, whom he knew. I told him to let them in, then come in himself, and wait. I also told him to bring his "Luger" 9mm Naval Parabellum. He had other handguns, but the "Luger" has a 6-inch barrel, which means accuracy. I told him to shoot anyone but me who showed a weapon. Not Alice, of course.

Then I called Bubba Antrim. His recording machine answered. I left the message: Pal Joey's tomorrow night at nine-thirty sharp.

There was one more call to make, the one I dreaded. I sat a while, sipping and smoking and thinking about Alice standing on a scaffold with a black hood over her head and a rope around her pretty neck, or sitting strapped to the electric chair, or in the gas chamber, waiting in horror for the whiff of cyanide, the long fall, the agonizing shock.

I picked up the phone and dialed Midtown North. When I had identified myself, the police operator gave me a number in Queens. A woman, undoubtedly the wife, answered. I told her who was calling, and I heard her yelling for Al. He grumbled his way to the phone.

"Heard from the girl, Streeter?" he growled.

"She'll be at the club tomorrow night at nine," I said. "What about the LA cops?"

"They're through," he said. "Gone already. Got nothing. You say tomorrow night? That's the Fourth. Okay, when she shows up, have her call me. Or *you* call. That's better."

"No," I said. "I want you to come to the club."

"Why's that, Streeter?"

"She won't talk to you directly."

"So, you've had a chance to talk to her about last night?"

"Yes," I said. "You're going to hear the story in her own words."

"Tell me *now.*"

"You wouldn't believe me."

"Just tell me what Charles Louis Urquhart was looking for when he burgled the girl's apartment," Sweeney said. "It was jewels, wasn't it?"

"Over four million dollars' worth."

"The loot from the Beverly Hills job?"

"You guessed it."

"And what's the girl's role?"

"We'll find out tomorrow night."

148

"You don't know?"

"I don't," I said. "I truly don't."

"But she's going to tell you. Is that it?"

"Yes."

"With *me* there?"

"No. You'll be downstairs in the greenroom, hearing it on a monitor. She and I will be in the club, at my private table. The sound system will be on. You should hear us very distinctly."

"Isn't that pretty elaborate, Streeter?"

"Not half as elaborate as her story's going to be. Now, I want you to enter the greenroom by way of the garden. Come to the garden through the alleyway alongside the building. You don't have to come alone, but try to be cool if you bring a squad. I'll leave the alley gate unlocked. There'll be someone in the greenroom to let you in."

"Who?"

"Stacy Brown, our jazz singer."

"She in on it?"

"On what?"

"With the other girl . . . the jewels . . ."

"Go back to sleep, good buddy. See you tomorrow night. Nine o'clock sharp. If you're late we'll start without you."

"How do you know she'll be there?"

"Stacy?"

"Alice, this María Los Angeles . . ."

"Trust me," I told him. "What could you lose?"

"Is she there now, Streeter?"

"No, of course not."

"Why of course not? Would you tell me if she was?"

"She's still in A.C., and I'd appreciate it if you'll call off your pickup-and-hold. Let her get back here with no hassles, will you?"

"All right," he said. "Tomorrow night. Nine o'clock.

You'd better come through, Streeter, or I swear to Jesus
. . . !''

I hung up wondering why he hadn't asked about Terence
D. Moran, for surely he'd tapped Moran's hospital phone.
Probably my phones too. No matter.

I rang the girls' apartment. Because of the late hour I had
to let it ring quite a few times. At length Stacy answered,
foggy with sleep. I asked her if she could be in the greenroom tomorrow night before nine to let someone in by the
garden door. She asked who. I said Lieutenant Sweeney.

"More trouble, Joey?"

"Probably."

"Is Alice all right?"

"Sleeping like an innocent child right now," I said.
"When Lieutenant Sweeney comes, I want you to wait in
the greenroom with him. Try to have Colleen and Caligari
there too."

"What about Herb?"

"He can't be there," I said. "Now, don't go to the greenroom through the club. Tell the others. Stay out of the
club."

"Why all the mystery, Joey?"

"I'm having a meeting," I explained, "with some heavies,
four of them. They all hate each other, and they hate me
most of all, or if they don't they will. A bystander could get
hurt."

"What about Alice?"

"What about her?"

"Will she be here? I mean . . .''

"She'll be with me," I said.

"But she could get hurt!"

"I'll see that she doesn't," I said. "You can count on that,
sugar. It's a promise. Now, get some sleep. And be in the
greenroom before nine tomorrow night, okay?"

"Okay. Take care of Alice."

I hung up, finished my drink, put the cigar in an ashtray, and went back to the bedroom. Alice was still sleeping soundly. I looked for her big snakeskin handbag. It lay on the floor by her side of the bed. I picked it up and opened it, hoping for Catherine's Egg, fearing I'd find the Spanish Dagger, but I found only a Colt "Detective Special" .38, fully loaded except for one empty cartridge. I emptied the gun, dropped the shells into the pocket of my robe, put the gun back in the snakeskin bag, and climbed into bed. Alice slept on. I lay awake a long time.

Shortly after first light I got up quietly, put on my robe, and went downstairs and unlocked the alley gate to the garden. Then I went back up to bed. Alice woke up. She wanted to make love. I couldn't.

15

We didn't go to Coney. On thinking it over, it seemed we'd be pressing our luck if I took her out now, for Sweeney had not said, after all, that he'd call off the pickup-and-hold, and he'd had more than enough time to realize that a skillful impersonator like Alice might easily be any woman he saw me with.

Otherwise it would have been a fine outing, one that Alice would remember. I would have rented the Harley again, and we'd have flown out to Coney Island. Hot dogs at Nathan's, half a dozen tickets on the Cyclone, and then the Wonder Wheel. That's the ride *suprême* if you have your girl along. Making it in one of those big cages when they start rocking high in the air can be maddening. Just thinking of it, I felt like a traitor. But who has never loved a madwoman? Some flatter themselves that they have not.

We'd thought of going swimming too, but I doubt that we would have. Too much sewage in the water. Of course, with the Harley we could have gone farther out, past the pollution, around Lido Beach. The mafiosi families there enjoy clean ocean water. Maybe there's a lesson in that? Anyway, making it in the ocean is one delight Alice and I never enjoyed together, and probably never will.

A good breakfast revived my nature, and we spent the day, on and off, in and out of bed. Betimes we prepared an elegant lunch, cold lobster and champagne. We didn't leave the apartment.

Along toward dinner time I asked Alice if she was hungry, and she said she was but she'd rather wait until after our meeting with Count Carlo. She'd eat better, once we concluded the arrangements for Carlota's Rosary.

At eight-thirty we went down to the club. I turned on the lights in the corner where I had my private table, and while I was doing that I also switched on the sound system and the tape recorder. In the low light Alice was unable to observe what I was doing. I told her to wait at the table while I went to the bar and got a bottle of champagne. I unlocked the street door, leaving it closed. We had half an hour to spend before our guests were due to arrive, first Lieutenant Sweeney at nine o'clock in the greenroom, then the others at nine-thirty. I put a Louis Armstrong cassette in the tape deck on the backbar, Louis playing solos with piano accompaniment, Duke Ellington, Oscar Peterson, and Earl Hines. Good-time jazz. Then I carried the champagne and a tray of hollow-stem glasses to the table. It was a magnum of Piper Heidsieck, and Alice clapped her hands with pleasure.

I drew the cork until it was ready to pop, then held the bottle for her while she popped it. We toasted each other in the golden bubbles.

"I love you," I told her.

"Oh, Joey!" she cried. "How touching! How sweet!"

But she didn't say, "I love you." Would it have made any difference if she had? And if she had, would it have been the truth?

"I'm going to level with you," I said. "And I want you to level with me."

"Always, Joey."

"Let's dance. We'll talk later."

And so we danced while Pops blew that sweet horn, slow dancing, more like fishing, as they say uptown. Pops sang "When Your Lover Has Gone," and I wished I'd never laid eyes on Alice. To lose a lover . . . It matters how. I couldn't think of a worse way to lose my lover than the way I was going to lose her. And so we danced, body to body, slowly, an act of love, for the last time.

At nine o'clock I said, "Let's sit out a few. We have to talk."

"All right," she said.

I refilled our glasses.

"I know what happened Saturday night," I told her. "I know all of it, what you did, and how you did it. What I don't know is why."

"What are you talking about, Joey?"

"Level with me, Alice. No more kidding around. I need to know why. I need to know everything."

"You said you love me, Joey. Do you, really?"

"Yes," I said. "I do."

"But if I tell you everything, you'll hate me."

"No."

"You will. I know you will."

"I don't hate."

"I hate myself!"

"I love you, baby," I said. "Believe me, it's not because you're good. I love you because you're lovable. You're also a liar, like everybody else, and a bad one. I do my share, too. But this is the moment of truth, sweetheart. I want the true story, all of it. I know that the Principessa Francesca di Casoli wasn't your mother. Her title goes back to a bastard son of Alexander the Sixth, the Borgia pope. The

154

principessa never was a Gómez nor a Farah, and you're not her daughter. The jewels are heirlooms, all right, but not your heirlooms. You weren't born in Mexico. You didn't attend UCLA. So tell me, sweet. Who are you, really? Where do you come from? I have a hunch you're a local girl. You let it slip last night when you said you hadn't been out to Coney in years. You haven't been that long in New York according to your original story. Now, how about the truth?"

"The truth?" she said, as if I'd asked her a hard one.

"Begin with your right name."

"I don't know my right name."

"Sweetheart . . .!"

"I'm an orphan, Joey."

She looked at me wide-eyed. Invincible innocence. Here we go, I thought, another ticket on the Cyclone. I refilled our glasses and settled back to enjoy the ride.

"Tell me about it, love."

She was a foundling, she said, and was raised at first in an orphanage. Later, because the nuns thought she looked like a Spanish child, she was given to a Puerto Rican couple, José Luis Farah, a longshoreman, and María Juana Gómez, a garment-factory machine operator. The Farah Gómezes lived in the Red Hook section of Brooklyn. They had no children of their own. Good Catholics, they named their adopted daughter María de los Ángeles. She attended parochial school in Red Hook. During her first semester at Brooklyn College her foster father fell into the hold of a ship and was killed. On being told about it, his wife had a stroke and died at her machine. There was life insurance, of course, through their unions, the ILA and the ILGWU.

She'd started calling herself Alice early in grade school because there were so many Marías in Red Hook. And she'd been into dramatics from the beginning, play-acting for as long as she could remember. She'd grabbed all the best roles in school plays, and during that first and only semester at Brooklyn College everybody knew a *real* actress was in their midst. While still in high school she'd gone to the Off-Broadway theater groups in Greenwich Village and quickly realized that amateur theatricals were not for her. School was out. She wanted to start as a pro. So she took her parents' life insurance money and bought a one-way ticket to the Coast, also a slick wardrobe. She'd give the cinema a break.

The money went fast, as it will when a poor girl from Red Hook gets a taste of the good life. She ended up with a hangover and a slick wardrobe. When the money was gone, she wrote a few checks, but not being stupid she could see that hanging paper leaves a trail, so she gave it up and moved in with a gentleman friend, an older man, a bartender on the Strip. He offered her a chance to make a lot of money quickly, and she accepted. All she had to do was drive the getaway car in a very cool jewel heist.

"You know the rest," she said.

I poured more champagne while I thought it over.

"No," I said. "I only know what happened here in New York. What happened before you came back to New York?"

"You want to know about the jewel robbery?" I said I did. "Well," she said, "I wasn't told any of the details beforehand. We drove to a place in Beverly Hills, and I waited in the car with the lights out and the motor running. It was a quiet street with very big homes. In a little while a lady and a gentleman got out of a taxi and walked to the front door of one of these homes. My partner stepped out of some bushes. He showed them the gun and took them inside. I waited and waited for him to come out. I couldn't understand what was taking so long. I was about to go and see what was wrong . . ."

I said, "You'd have gone in after him?"

"Of course," she said.

156

"You weren't afraid?"

"Naturally I was afraid. What's that got to do with it? Anyway he came out then. He took his time walking to the car, and then he handed me a black bag like the kind doctors carry. He told me to wait. He didn't explain, he just went back in the house. He was gone for a long time again, and I spent the time looking at the things in the black bag. The light was poor, but I could see enough. Joey, you have no idea! The Egg! You have to see it to believe it!"

"I believe it," I said. "What happened then?"

"Well, then he came out of the house again and got in the car. He said to drive away slowly. I did. We didn't want to get busted for a traffic violation, he said, with four million dollars worth of jewels in the car. He said it wasn't his car, either. I was sick to my stomach with anxiety all the way back to his place."

"So far, so good," I said. "You've told me how you got the Egg, the Rosary, the Dagger, and the ruby ring. Right?"

"Yes," she said. "It's the truth, Joey. It happened just the way I told you."

"Now tell me," I said, "how *you* got away with the loot."

"The next morning," she said, "my partner went to bring some people to view the jewels . . ."

"Your partner being Terence D. Moran?"

"You guessed!"

"Why did you pull a blank when I brought up his name before?"

"Oh, Joey! Do we have to go over all that? It's different now. We're in this together."

"Go ahead," I said. "Moran went to bring some people to view the jewels."

"Yes," she said. "But he only brought one, Count Carlo."

"The other was being held as a material witness, right?"

"Yes, but I almost quit then, before they got back," she

157

said. "While Moran was out I listened to the news on the radio. There wasn't any TV in his pad. The big news was about the jewel robbery in Beverly Hills, and that's when I first found out what happened in that house, what took so long . . . I was getting ready to leave, with the jewels, when Moran returned with Count Carlo. Believe me, Joey, you don't know what scared is! I didn't know what to make of the count, but Moran was a killer, a rape-murderer, a strangler. I had to get away from him, but I couldn't find a way."

"But you did find a way," I pointed out.

"It took a while," she said. "I had no money. Neither had Moran. He borrowed a hundred from Count Carlo, but that's all the fat little dago would give him. So that afternoon Moran told me he'd thought of a way to get a few grand with no effort and no waiting around. All I'd have to do was drive the car again. I didn't want to do it, but I was afraid not to. I think he would have killed me if I'd refused, or even hung back a little. You couldn't tell by looking, Joey, but he was crazy, stark, raving mad. All in a quiet way. No, not raving. It was the things he said, sort of . . . You know, like out of left field?"

"So you went along," I said. "Did he get the money?"

"I didn't know where we were going, Joey. He said never mind, when I asked him, just drive the car and shut up. I didn't know it was a bank until I let him out of the car and he went in. Even then, I didn't know for sure what he was going to do. Then I heard gunshots, and he came running out of the bank with a bag in one hand and two guns in the other. We got away with seventy-five hundred dollars. He was wounded in his left leg, but it wasn't bad, and I patched it up when we got back to his place."

"You're not telling me," I said, "how you got away with the loot, the jewels."

"Yes, I am," she said. "The next morning Moran's leg

was stiff and sore. He could hardly get out of bed. So I just picked up the black bag and split."

"You also took the money, Moran's wallet and ID, and the detective's gun."

"Joey, you peeked!"

I admired her spirit. Of course, now that we were in this together, and all that . . . To make a long story longer wasn't possible, because it was suddenly show time.

Bubba Antrim came in the street door and straight back to my table. Alice was surprised to see him, of course, but she said nothing. I told her I'd thought it would be well to have a witness, and she seemed to agree. Bubba was very courtly. He kissed her hand and told her how marvelous he'd thought her performance the other night. I poured him a glass of champagne.

Count Carlo arrived then. I gave him the same explanation that I'd given Alice for Bubba's presence, and he seemed to accept it. He too was very courtly, bowing over Alice's hand and complimenting her in his richest Roman accent. Alice seemed unsure of her role, for once nonplussed.

We were just sitting down when Terence D. Moran walked in. He was the tall man I'd seen on the videotape. No doubt about it now. He was at least six feet four and weighed a good two hundred forty. If *he'd* been Count Carlo's partner, instead of Charles Louis Urquhart, the fight for the knife might have gone the other way. He looked like a Green Bay guard or a professional wrestler. Broken nose. Knuckle scars around his eyes. Thick lips.

He came back to the table without saying anything. He just walked slowly, his right hand in his coat pocket, and looked us over as he came. I introduced him to Bubba. He knew the others. He ignored my introduction.

"What the hell's going on here?" he demanded.

Alice picked her snakeskin handbag off the floor by her

chair and put it in her lap. I unbuttoned my jacket. Count Carlo was holding one hand behind his back. Evidently he wore his gun on his hip. His second gun. I had his first.

"You said this would be a viewing, Mr. Streeter," he complained. "You have tricked me into coming here."

Moran said, "Yeah. That's right. Something's wrong here. What's it all about, buddy?"

"I'm expecting one more," I said.

"Who's that?" Moran asked.

"I don't think you know him," I said. "I doubt that Count Carlo would have let you meet his buyer."

"Pearse!" cried Carlo. "He's coming *here?*"

His right shoulder twitched. I thought he was going for his gun, but he didn't. I could have stopped him, had he tried.

Moran said, "You told me we was gonna go someplace and get them jewels, buddy. What kind of a game you playin'?"

"The jewels are here," I said.

"So let's see 'em," Moran said.

"I'll show you one of them," I said, "as an earnest."

"An earnest," said Moran. "What the hell's that?"

I reached down and took Alice's left arm by the wrist and raised her hand for them all to see the ruby ring. I don't think Moran recognized it, jewelry was just jewelry to him, but Count Carlo did.

"Very well," he said. "But I did not come to view my own work, Mr. Streeter."

"You got everything, Streeter," asked Moran, "the Egg and the Rosary and the Dagger, the whole bag?" I said I had. "Okay," he said. "How about we don't wait for this colonel fella. Let me just take the Rosary for my share, and I'll be on my way. What say?"

Alice hadn't said a word since Moran came in, but now she leaped to her feet, eyes blazing, and shouted, "You sack

160

of shit! You want the Rosary?" She raised her dress high. "Let's see if you're man enough to take it!" Everyone was staring at Carlota's Rosary, wrapped once around Alice's waist, pearls gleaming against her skin, silver Christ hanging in her dark bush. She lowered her dress. Moran hadn't moved. Alice said, "Maybe you'd like the Dagger instead? I gave it to you once, turkey! You want me to give it to you again?"

She reached into her handbag. Carlo reached for his hip. He got the gun out before I could stop him, but I grabbed his hand and twisted it out of his fingers. It fired accidentally as I took it away from him. Matt suddenly appeared in the doorway, "Luger" in hand. Moran was pulling a snub-nose .38 out of his coat pocket, a dumb place to keep a gun. Alice had got the Colt "Detective Special" out of her handbag and was pointing it at Moran and pulling the trigger on empty chambers. Moran had his .38 out now, but it flew out of his hand as Matt's big 9mm "Luger" roared. Some of Moran's hand flew away with it. He screamed and doubled up with pain. Flesh wounds often don't hurt right away, but a bone shot is pure agony. Lucky Moran got it in the hand, for I was ready to put one in his rotten brain when Matt drew down on him.

Suddenly Sweeney popped up through the trapdoor in the stage with gun in hand.

"Thanks, Streeter," he said.

He went to work putting cuffs on Alice, Moran, and Count Carlo. Only then did Bubba Antrim come out from under the table. Sweeney read the rights and arrested the three on conspiracy to commit murder, namely their complicity in the murder of the Principessa di Casoli. He gave Moran special mention for the rape-strangling and for the killing of the LA cop. Sweeney spoke on for a while, citing grand theft, transporting stolen goods across state lines, receiving stolen goods, and on and on.

161

Alice was livid with fury. She did nothing as yet, but she was looking at me as if I were dog meat. She knew how to hate. For a moment I wondered how I could have been so sentimental about her.

Then I told Sweeney, "Send Moran and Carlo on down. We have a little business with Alice."

"Yes?"

"Another homicide."

He went to the street door and brought in a squad. They took Carlo and Moran away.

"There's another stiff upstairs," I told Sweeney. "It's Herb Junep. He was our comic. Alice knocked him on the head, then stabbed him with the Spanish Dagger, early yesterday morning."

"You son of a bitch!" she shrieked. She tried to get at me, but her wrists were cuffed behind her. "You can't prove I did it!"

Sweeney said, "Can you, Streeter?"

"I can," I said.

Caligari came up through the trapdoor then, followed by Stacy and Colleen, more curious than scared. They looked at Alice, sitting at the table with her hands manacled behind her.

She said, "I suppose everybody heard everything I told you, you bastard!"

Sweeney said, "That we did, girlie. And these here are my witnesses."

"There's also a tape," I said.

"Well, now," Sweeney said, "that's very professional of you, Streeter. And I'm much obliged."

"Maybe you'll fix a speeding ticket for me?" I said. "They'll be coming to Buster's Bike Shop looking for the man on the Harley."

"No problem," he said. "You were assisting me in an investigation."

162

"Why don't you two cops kiss and get it on?" Alice said.

Stacy went to her, put an arm around her, and said, "You poor kitten!"

Alice let herself be comforted, a cuddly kitten with eight small razors hidden in her soft little paws.

Sweeney said, "You were going to prove something for me, Streeter?" He slowly drew a White Owl out of his handkerchief pocket. I took the hint and gave him a Brazilian. When he'd lit it, he said to Alice, "Girlie, how about it? Did you kill this comedian, Herb Junep?"

"Certainly not," she said.

"How about it, Streeter?"

"She also killed, or tried to kill, Charles Louis Urquhart."

"Boy!" said Alice. "Dig the Sherlock Holmes! You should go on TV or something, you know that, Joey?"

"She also jimmied the back window of my apartment," I said, "breaking in . . ."

Sweeney said, "Add burglary to the other charges. Girlie, when you go, you really go, don't you?"

"I didn't steal anything in Joey's apartment," she said.

"That's true," I told Sweeney. "She didn't break in to steal something. She had something to hide, and she was in a hurry. Two things, in fact." Alice was watching me warily. I knew the whole story, and she knew I knew it, though she didn't know how. "I'll show you," I said, "how Alice managed to shoot Urquhart in the back, stab Moran in the chest, and murder Herb Junep, and I'll show you how no one else could have done it."

16

"I've sent for a matron to take that Rosary off of her," Sweeney said.

"Don't let a little thing like modesty impede swift justice," I told him. I lifted Alice off her chair, raised her dress above her lovely bottom, and unhooked the Rosary. "Here," I said, handing it to Sweeney. "You can take the ring off her finger yourself."

"What about those other things?" he asked. "That big Egg and the fancy Dagger?"

"I'll explain about them," I said. "The thing to bear in mind, now, is the timing. Only Alice could have been on the fire escape shooting at Urquhart, or in Junep's bathroom knocking him on the head with an old tire iron she found in the tool drawer of my kitchen. Here's how she did it."

"Joey," she said. "Joey?"

I looked at her. She looked pitiful. I swear to God it seemed to me all wrong to be doing this to her. I had to remind myself that the girl had murdered a man. She'd *tried* to murder three men. I believe that sooner or later she'd have tried to murder me, perhaps when she'd got her money for Carlota's Rosary and was ready to run off with the $3,500,000 Catherine's Egg. At that point she might have given me the $50,000 Spanish Dagger, a consolation prize, though in fact she'd already given it to Moran and Junep and hadn't left it with them. But she did indeed look pitiful, hunched over in her chair, with her hands manacled behind her. Stacy, Colleen, and Caligari stood staring at me as if I were the Grand Inquisitor tormenting a poor heretic. Bubba seemed to understand, for he knew more than they did. Sweeney simply waited for me to get on with it. I told Caligari to go to the bar and get another magnum of Piper Heidsieck and more glasses.

"As you all know," I said, "Alice first disappeared at about twelve forty-five Sunday morning, during the magic show. She'd seen Terence Moran in the audience. I saw him on the videotape of one of the crowd shots. At first I thought Alice had panicked and run away, but in fact she was running after Moran. To try and kill him. She disguised herself as a Times Square hooker, using makeup and wardrobe in the greenroom, and she left the building by way of the garden and the alleyway. As she was running through the alley she met Count Carlo and Charles Louis Urquhart, whom she knew from the Beverly Hills jewel robbery. Neither of them was really heavy, and she got past them, but not before they'd taken her apartment keys and Moran's wallet with his ID. She was wearing Carlota's Rosary around her waist, under her dress, as you all saw just now. She was not carrying Catherine's Egg, or they would have found it. And she hadn't hidden it in her apartment, for they tossed the place very thoroughly. Obviously she'd already hidden it elsewhere, probably in Herb Junep's apartment. She was carrying the Colt "Detective Special" thirty-eight that she tried to shoot Moran with a few minutes ago. I emptied the gun last night."

"Where is it?" Sweeney asked. "Where's that gun?" He'd grabbed her handbag and was rummaging through it. "That's the gun killed a cop in Los Angeles. What did you do with it?"

Alice ignored him. What could she say? I told him to look under the table. She'd probably dropped it there when he popped up from the greenroom. He looked, and found it. I went on with the sequence of events involving Alice.

"I know from the videotape," I said, "that Moran was in the club during Alice's performance and left right after her disappearance. I think she was going after him but ran into Carlo and Urquhart instead. When they took her keys she had to follow them by way of the garden and then the fire escape ladders to her floor. By then Carlo and Urquhart had entered her apartment, opened the bedroom window as an emergency escape route, and were ransacking the rooms. I came in the hall door about that time. Urquhart attacked me with the Spanish Dagger. We fought. As I forced the blade into him, Alice fired a shot from the fire escape, hitting Urquhart in the back."

"No!" Alice cried. "I was trying to help *you*, Joey!"

"Thanks, love," I said. "I wondered later why you hadn't waited and picked off Carlo too. I figured you needed him to sell the jewels for you, whereas Urquhart was merely an unnecessary partner and therefore expendable. You could have shot me too, and that puzzled Lieutenant Sweeney before he learned tonight that it was you who shot Urquhart.

"You bastard!" Alice whispered. Hunched over, with her hands cuffed behind her, she looked like a trussed up wild animal. She all but snarled and hissed. "You fucking, lousy bastard!"

"The way I jumped in with both feet," I said, "you must have realized right away that I was on your side, that I'd do whatever I could to help you handle those two baddies,

Carlo and Moran. Anyway, Moran wasn't on the scene for you to eliminate. And you thought you'd need Carlo. So you waited on the fire escape, probably on the floor below, until you saw Carlo come out of the window and go up to the roof with me after him. You waited until I returned and went back into your apartment. You watched me from the bedroom window, and when I left the apartment by the hall door you went in and took the Spanish Dagger out of Charles, wiped off the blade on his jacket, and stowed it in that big snakeskin handbag. Then you went down the ladders to my back porch, then the stairs to the garden, and out through the alleyway to the street. Carlo had gone over the roofs and out to the street through another building, unless he was waiting in one of the buildings until he was sure he wasn't being ambushed. He knew Moran was a psycho, and he must have feared not only him but you too, and for the same reason." Alice's eyes were staring mad with some emotion I couldn't fathom. Hatred maybe. I'm not sure it was an emotion at all. "When you hit the street," I said, "you looked for Carlo and saw Moran. You went after him, but you couldn't kill him on the street. Cops would be coming along very soon. So you made like nice, and the two of you went over to Houlihan's saloon in Hell's Kitchen. There you took him into the ladies' room, like any Hell's Kitchen hooker, and there you stabbed him. You must have hit a rib. You put a hurt on him, but not a good one, so you had to run. He had to go to the hospital. Now, here's the thing, and it fits you, baby, like it was tailor made. You disappear at twelve forty-five, shoot Urquhart in the back a little before one-thirty, and stab Moran very amateurishly at about two o'clock. In one of my books of quotations an old Roman poet says *Tempus edax rerum*. It means that time destroys all things. Time has certainly destroyed you, sweetheart. Only you could have done what you did and at those times and where you did them."

Sweeney said, "What about this Herb Junep?"

"At two-thirty," I said, "Alice reappeared here as Harriet Maxwell, the Times Square hooker from Brooklyn. We went upstairs, and I questioned her. She told me some lies. I knew she was lying, but I wasn't particularly interested. Lying is a way of life. It's the civilized way . . ."

Sweeney said, "Never mind the philosophy, Streeter. Get to the stiff upstairs."

"You came and woke us up," I told him, "at six in the morning. You told me a number of interesting things, showed me some computer printouts, all about the jewel robbery and rape-murder in Beverly Hills and the bank robbery and cop killing in Los Angeles. When you left, I went back to the bedroom. Alice had disappeared again. I went looking for her. This was around seven o'clock. I didn't find her. I found Junep instead, lying in his bathtub with a big knife wound in his chest. He hadn't been dead long. The water was still hot. I found a bloody spot on the back of his head. The blood was not yet dry. One bedroom window was open. The other had an air-conditioner going full blast. I figured his killer had come in through the hall door and left through the bedroom window. Junep had let the killer in, someone he knew. It had to be Alice, though I didn't want to see it then. The others were all accounted for, Caligari sleeping off a hangover, Stacy and Colleen having breakfast. And the timing was right. Needless to add, there was no knife sticking in Junep's chest. I left his apartment the way the killer had, by the bedroom window. I went down to the parlor floor, intending to return to my place by the back porch door. I noticed that one of the porch windows had been jimmied. An odd thing about the jimmy marks . . ."

Sweeney said, "I knew it! They were fresh. They didn't show any weathering."

"No," I said. "The odd thing about the jimmy marks

didn't strike me until later, when I nailed the windows shut. The marks on the sill were much larger than those ordinarily made by a burglar's jimmy. I think they were made by an old tire iron that I keep in the tool drawer in my kitchen."

"Did you check it out?" Sweeney asked.

"No. You can do that. I knew all I needed to know by then, as far as the jimmied window was concerned. Nothing had been stolen from the apartment. So why would someone break in?"

Sweeney said, "They were looking for the jewels. They thought Alice had hidden them in *your* apartment, since they didn't find them in hers when they burgled it."

"Or someone was trying to hide something," I said. "With a jimmied window you naturally assume burglary is the motive. The opposite was the case. Alice had gone to Herb Junep's apartment to retrieve something she'd hidden there, and then she'd broken into my place to hide it again. Herb must have given her an argument."

"You've got it all wrong, Joey. It wasn't like that," Alice said. "It's true, I did eavesdrop on your talk with Lieutenant Sweeney, and I was frightened, so I went to see Herbie. When I told him what was happening, he tried to take advantage of me. Joey, he tried to rape me!"

"Backwards, sweetheart?"

"Joey, don't!"

"He had a bloody place on the *back* of his head where you slugged him with a tire iron. Was he trying to rape you backwards? And what was he doing in the bathtub while he was trying to rape you?"

"You don't understand! You're not *trying*, Joey! Why are you doing this to me?"

Her wonderful cool was gone, all gone now. She went through scenes of love or hate without control. Wild fury followed pitiful pleading. I didn't believe any of it. At the

169

heart of all her personae there was no María de los Ángeles, only Alice. And who was she?

I told Sweeney to send a couple of men to look in the water tank above my john; they'd probably find Catherine's Egg and the Spanish Dagger.

Alice tried again, tears flowing down her lovely cheeks, "Joey! Get me off the hook, Joey! Please! You can't just throw me away now. You gave me my break, love. I belong to you. Don't throw me away, Joey!"

She got out of her chair and came to me, all the way, pressing her body against mine, her hands locked behind her. She looked up into my eyes, her own full of tears, and I swear I regretted everything I had done, but I couldn't regret one thing, loving her.

I told Sweeney, "You'd better send her down now."

He told a couple of his men to take her out to the car. He asked if Moran and Count Carlo had been taken to the precinct yet. He was told that they were being held outside. A couple of inspectors from Internal Affairs were questioning them.

We heard a string of explosions from somewhere outside, loud enough to make all of us jump, and Sweeney said, "Fourth of July freaks."

A cop came running in, yelling for Sweeney to come out, somebody shot one of the prisoners. Sweeney stood where he was.

"Which prisoner?" he asked the man.

"The little fat guy," the cop said. "We saw the gunman. He got away in a limousine with a chauffeur. It had New York plates. One of the men got the number. Two cars went after the limo, but they lost a little time when they ran into each other, pulling away from the curb."

"Questioning prisoners on the open sidewalk," said Sweeney. "Maybe Internal Affairs should investigate their own people. Incompetence!"

I said, "Count Carlo was your link to Colonel Pearse. Looks like the colonel broke the link. Too bad. I was working on a theory that he was behind the Beverly Hills jewel heist. He was up against the Principessa di Casoli about a year and a half ago in an auction at the Sotheby Parke Bernet galleries, and she outbid him on two items, Carlota's Rosary and the Spanish Dagger. He was prepared to buy both items from me, plus Catherine's Egg, and I expected him to come tonight."

"Looks like he did," Sweeney said. "I take it Alice and this fellow Moran don't know Colonel Pearse?"

"Probably not," I said. "I think he only dealt with Count Carlo. But you may be able to get your teeth into him anyway. He keeps an American eagle in an aviary at his estate on Heliotrope Lane in Glen Cove. The bald eagle is an endangered species, and keeping one without a permit is a felony. Start with that, you may work up to something. You'd better get Moran and Alice down to the precinct before worse things happen."

He gave the order, and two of his men took Alice by the arms. She hung back, staring wordlessly at me.

Then with a look of utter loathing she said, slowly and with great venom, "Joe Streeter, you play lousy piano. You're just a dirty old man!"

The anticlimax was too much. I almost wanted to laugh. If I didn't it's because there was something in my throat. My heart, I think.

The cops took her away. She went off laughing. It was the eeriest sound I'd ever heard.

171

17

I gave Sweeney the tape recording of my dialogue with Alice in which she recounted the Beverly Hills jewel robbery and murder and the subsequent bank robbery and cop-killing. He had the rest of it, also, my reduction of Alice's homicidal activities to a time schedule that only she could have managed.

"That wraps it up," I told him, "except for Bubba Antrim's piece in tomorrow morning's paper. You're the hero of the hour. You could make Cop of the Year."

"What about *you?*" Sweeney said. "I don't want him writing about you obstructing justice, withholding evidence. Internal Affairs would love to get me that way."

"He'll protect you," I said. "That right, Bubba?"

"Right," said Bubba. "Whatever you say. But I'd dearly love to tell the whole story, how we went to Count Carlo's apartment, what you did there, and all that."

"Keep me out of it," I said. "Let Lieutenant Sweeney play Sherlock Holmes. If anything at all, let me play Dr. Watson, his humble admirer. Whatever I did, in my small

172

way, was done under the lieutenant's direction. He master-minded the entire investigation."

"I could wish so many people didn't know about it," Sweeney said.

Caligari, Stacy, and Colleen were lingering about, watching and listening. Caligari nonchalantly lit a cigarette.

Stacy said, "Come on, Colleen, let's rehearse."

The two girls went up on the stage. Caligari poured himself another glass of champagne.

"I don't think you need worry about them," I told Sweeney. "Show people gossip a lot. But who believes them? The official story will be Bubba's version in tomorrow morning's paper."

"Which reminds me," Bubba said. "I've got a deadline. If something new develops, call me at the paper."

"I'll be calling you," Sweeney said. "I want a copy of your column before it goes to press."

"Don't call me, Lieutenant. Let me call you. I'll read you the copy over the phone. You can make whatever corrections then."

"You can reach me through Midtown Precinct North," said Sweeney. "And I appreciate what you're doing."

They shook hands, and Bubba left. An assistant medical examiner arrived with two morgue attendants carrying a stretcher. Sweeney told them which apartment Junep was in and sent them upstairs.

When they were gone, Sweeney said, "Well, Streeter, it looks like I owe you one."

"At least," I said.

"Internal Affairs will be interrogating me any time now," he said. "They'll want to know who shot Count Carlo."

"You'll tell them," I said. "You're continuing the investigation, and Colonel John Patrick Pearse is your next suspect."

"You could lend a hand," he said.

173

"How's that?"

"Help me get this Colonel Pearse."

"Sorry," I said. "I don't think he can be had. Too rich. Too many rich connections. You can get him for the bald eagle, but not on conspiracy to commit a murder. With Carlo dead, there's no provable culpability, so far as I know. But maybe you'll uncover something."

"Are you saying you won't help me?"

"I'm saying something like that, yes."

"In the interests of justice, Streeter?"

"*Really,* Sweeney!"

"Too corny for you?"

"It doesn't concern me."

"It did, though, didn't it?"

"Of course it did. At first I hoped there might be an out for Alice. After Junep's murder I knew there wasn't. I have no further interest in this case. I'd like to see you nail Pearse, but I don't believe it can be done, and I'm not going to waste my precious time pounding sand into ratholes."

"Tell me something," Sweeney said. "Weren't you after the jewels?"

"As Confucius said, money is just something you have to live with."

"That's an answer?"

"Think about it."

"Did you sleep with that girl?"

"Alice? Yes, of course."

"With a murderess? My God, you must have nerves of ice!"

"Not at all. It added a certain piquancy to the experience. Try it sometime."

"But you knew you were going to turn her in," Sweeney said. "How could you sleep with her, knowing that?"

"It bothered me," I said. "I had visions of her hanging by her neck until dead, frying in the hot seat, gagging in the gas chamber. But thinking soberly, we both know she won't get the death penalty. She'll go away for a while, federal time for conspiracy to commit the bank job, transporting stolen goods across state lines. But federal time, as everybody since Watergate knows, is a picnic in the country."

"But then she'll have to face murder charges in California and New York," said Sweeney. "She'll go away for life."

"Even life has parole," I reminded him. "Besides, she may never face murder charges. The bank robbery and transporting charges take precedence. She could walk away from a federal prison looking like one of the matrons."

"And then she'll come looking for *you*, right?"

"With blood in her eye," I said. "And that's called the "Crazy Woman Blues." But let her come. I'll take my chances. Let me tell you something, old buddy, and you should think about it. I don't know if you're ready for this, but I shall always love her."

Sweeney wagged his head despairingly, and as he left to go out and face the Internal Affairs inspectors, he delivered a parting shot.

"You're well rid of her, Streeter. Young broads are trouble."

I told Caligari to break out more champagne. We'd have a party. He and Matt went to the bar, and I went to the piano. Stacy was singing "Going to Chicago Blues" while Colleen did a soft-shoe shuffle. When I started playing accompaniment, Stacy began to improvise a lyric:

> Got me a crazy woman,
> Crazy as a broad can be!
> Got me a crazy woman,
> Crazy as a broad can be!
> Gun-totin' crazy woman
> Gonna be the death of me!

Later, when we were all in the club kitchen preparing a midnight snack, Stacy said, "You should hang out more with your own generation, Joey."

"I know," I said. "Alice was pretty young. She made up for her youth with a lot of experience."

"How old are you, Joey?"

"Forty-nine."

"How long you been forty-nine, honey?"

"Not too long."

"Would you believe, I'm forty?"

"I'd have said thirty, or less."

"Is that over the hill, sugar?"

"Certainly not, Stacy. You look just fine."

"I'm not too old for *you?*"

"No."

"Or too young?"

"No."

There was more of that, but I didn't take her up on it. For one thing, it could wait. For another, I had a lot of thinking to do, about Alice and what she'd meant to me, why I got involved with a girl thirty years younger, above all how come I got hooked by a crazy woman.

The following morning I went early to an AKC pet shop down on 14th Street, where I'd bought Schatzi, and I found a silvery shepherd pup. Twelve weeks old. There were five in the litter, but she seemed to try harder than the others to get to me. I paid the money and picked her up.

"We're going home, Schatzi."

She kissed the tip of my nose. It was love at first sight.

ROSS THOMAS

The Fools in Town are on Our Side

'What kind of money?' I said.

'The fifty thousand kind.'

'That is a nice kind. What do I have to do to earn it?'

'What I want you to do, Mr Dye, is to corrupt me a city.'

Kicked out of Section 2, an obscure branch of the American Intelligence Service, friendless, displaced and almost without an identity, Lucifer C. Dye accepts.

And he has little difficulty, as the town is already a hotbed of corruption! Allying himself to various criminal factions he embarks on a fascinating series of double and even double-double crosses. The result: all-out gang warfare from which Lucifer C. Dye is pushed to emerge with his life!

JAMES M. CAIN

Galatea

Holly is a grossly overweight side-show freak. The devious and evil Valentry is her husband. He is just waiting for her to die to get his hands on her wealth . . .

Duke Webster is the man Holly loves, the misfit from the West, a jailbird on loan to the Valentrys as a manual worker. Soon his attention turns to the fat and miserable Mrs Valentry, whom he helps to become stunningly beautiful. She is devoted to her saviour and when he suggests leaving her husband to go away with him, she is more than willing. But Valentry isn't going to let her go. He decides to trick the eloping couple – and kill them afterwards. But the trick misfires – and backfires . . .

A superbly suspenseful story from the master of crime James M. Cain, author of *The Institute* and *The Postman Always Rings Twice*.

ELLIS PETERS

A Morbid Taste for Bones

The possession of suitable saintly relics will add much prestige to the great Benedictine monastery at Shrewsbury. Brother Cadfael leaves his precious herb-gardens to join the party travelling to a remote village to bring back the bones of an obscure Welsh saint. But the local villagers resent the loss of their beloved little saint. Tempers mount and before long murder is committed. Then it's up to Brother Cadfael to track down the murderer before he strikes again . . .

ELLIS PETERS

One Corpse Too Many

In the grisly aftermath of the Battle of Shrewsbury in 1138, Brother Cadfael leaves his peaceful monastery to undertake the harrowing work of burying the dead.

The official tally of the slain is 94 – but Brother Cadfael finds he has 95 to bury . . .

In this matter of the 'corpse too many'. Brother Cadfael's extraordinary abilities are taxed to the limit. He has to rtack down a murderer and avenge a brutal death.

Also available in Magnum Books

JAMES MELVILLE
Wages of Zen

Murder cases which are not part of gang warfare or private family are rare in Japan. When Superintendent Otani is called in to investigate a murder in a Buddhist Community, the problem of motive is a difficult one to determine. And the case calls for delicate handling as Europeans are among the suspects.

The clues begin to point in the direction of heroin trafficking, the politics of Japanese organised crime – and Otani is faced with a local crime leading to international terrorism and extreme danger . . .

Superintendent Otani is a delightful addition to the world of detective fiction.

More top Crime from Magnum Books

These and other Magnum Books are available at your bookshop or newsagent. In case of difficulties orders may be sent to:

> Magnum Books
> Cash Sales Department
> P.O. Box 11
> Falmouth
> Cornwall TR10 109EN

Please send cheque or postal order, no currency, for purchase price quoted and allow the following for postage and packing:

U.K. 40p for first book, plus 18p for the second book and 13p for each additional book ordered to a maximum charge of £1.49p.

B.F.P.O. & Eire 40p for the first book, plus 18p for the second book and 13p per copy for the next 7 books, thereafter 7p per book.

Overseas Customers 60p for the first book, plus 18p per copy for each additional book.

While every effort is made to keep prices low, it is sometimes necessary to increase prices at short notice. Magnum Books reserves the right to show new retail prices on covers which may differ from those previously advertised in the text or elsewhere.